Marco & Rakia 3:

Not Your Ordinary Hood Love

Tina J

Copyright 2020

Warning:

This book is strictly Urban Fiction and the story is **NOT**

REAL!

Characters will not behave the way you want them to; nor will

they react to situations the way you think they should. Some of

them may be drug addicts, kingpins, savages, thugs, rich, poor,

ho's, sluts, haters, bitter ex-girlfriends or boyfriends, people

from the past and the list can go on and on. That is what Urban

Fiction mostly consists of. If this isn't anything you foresee

yourself interested in, then do yourself a favor and don't read it

because it's only going to piss you off. ☺☺

Also, the book will not end the way you want so please be

advised that the outcome will be based solely on my own

thoughts and ideas. Thanks so much to my readers, supporters,

publisher and fellow authors and authoress for the support.

Author Tina J

Caught Up Loving A Beast 1, 2 & 3

A Street King And His Shawty 1 & 2

I Fell For The Wrong Bad Boy 1&2

I Wanna Love You 1 & 2

Addicted to Loving a Boss 1, 2, & 3

I Need That Gangsta Love 1&2

Creepin With The Plug 1 & 2

All Eyes On The Crown 1,2&3

When She's Bad, I'm Badder: Jiao and Dreek, A Crazy

Love Story 1,2&3

Still Luvin A Beast 1&2

Her Man, His Savage 1 & 2

Marco & Rakia: Not Your Ordinary, Hood Kinda Love 1,2

& 3

Feenin For A Real One 1, 2 & 3

A Kingpin's Dynasty 1, 2 & 3

What Kinda Love Is This: Captivating A Boss 1, 2 & 3

Frankie & Lexi: Luvin A Young Beast 1, 2 & 3

A Dope Boys Seduction 1, 2 & 3

My Brother's Keeper 1. 2 & 3

C'Yani & Meek: A Dangerous Hood Love 1, 2 & 3

When A Savage Falls for A Good Girl 1, 2 & 3

Eva & Deray 1 & 2

Blame It On His Gangsta Luv 1 & 2

Falling for The Wrong Hustla 1, 2 & 3

I Gave My Heart to A Jersey Killa 1, 2 & 3

Luvin The Son of a Savage 1, 2 & 3

A Dopeman and His Shawty 1, 2 & 3

Somebody Else's Thug 1, 2 & 3

Can't Trust Them Thugs 1, 2 &3

Previously…

Cara

As I stood over my grandmothers' casket, letting the tears fall, all I could think of, is how I let her down. All she wanted, was for me to make up with Rakia and apologize to her. Unfortunately, her man isn't gonna allow me to live, whether I apologize or not. He already had people looking for me and I know that, because his father, told my mom. It wasn't that I hated Rakia, I just hated the fact she got the man of my dreams. Why couldn't he love me the way her loved her? Why didn't he take the time out to get to know me? What was it about me, that is any different from her, besides being smart. I was gorgeous, had a nice body and would've done anything for him, had he given me a chance. But all of it is out the window, and now that my grandmother is gone, I'm gonna finish off what I started with Rakia. The bitch is going to find out Marco's little secret, he doesn't want her to know.

Yea, my mom told me they were over at the repast. She also mentioned, how she tried to tell Rakia before the funeral and again, right before they went into the repast. However, he blocked her from doing it both times. See, I learned a few things about Marco, from Bobbi and Mia. One… he loved sex. Two… Mia, was his first true love but coming back didn't work out the way she planned. And three… he would do anything for my cousin; including kill.

I admit, my ass cried a little, when I found out she was pregnant. My grandmother was ecstatic to be having two great grandchildren. We found out, not too long ago about Rahmel's chick expecting. It's too bad, she passed first. She would've been mad for me telling Marco's secret anyway, but who cares? She's been upset with me all this time; another few months wouldn't have hurt from her not speaking. I'm sure she's turning in her grave already knowing what I'm about to do.

On the drive over to the repast, Bobbi and I, smoked two blunts. At least, if I died, I'd be high. We stayed in the car until my mother came out. She told us where Rakia was sitting and how Marco wasn't allowing her outta his sight. The only way to get close to her, would be in the bathroom. She told us, she'd let us know, when she went in there. Being pregnant, meant using it a lot.

About ten minutes later, we got the text and both of us ran in through the back. My mom opened the door and we slid straight to the bathroom. You could see how crowded it was and I saw Tech and Marco, talking. My mom stood outside the door to tell people, it was broken and she was waiting on someone to unclog the toilet. The moment Rakia, stepped out the stall, I could see fear and sadness on her face. *Boy, was this gonna be fun.*

"Hey cousin. Long time, no see." She looked past me at Bobbi.

"Hi Cara, I didn't see you at the funeral. Did you like the service?" She grabbed a paper towel after washing her hands.

"It was nice. Anyway, I see your neck and arm healed up." I tried to touch it and she backed up.

"What do you want Cara?" I smirked and turned to look at Bobbi, who was doing the same.

"We wanna know." I pointed back and forth between, me and Bobbi.

"We wanna know, why you stole our man?"

"Cara, I didn't steal him from you and you know it. As far as this other woman, I didn't even know about her until the street party and he said, he wasn't with her."

"And you believed him?"

"Why wouldn't I?" She tried to move past, so I blocked her. I heard a tap on the door. My mom was telling me, either I was taking too long, or he was coming.

"Just like the gullible chick you are. He was still messing with both of us." She shook her head laughing.

"He stopped messing with Bobbi, and we all know it, because he called her out in front of me." I looked at Bobbi, who shrugged her shoulders. The dumb bitch didn't even tell me.

"I know about the two of you, in New York. All you did was give him head and he didn't like it. He left and you tried again, so he let you and then, on the way to Jersey. He blocked you and you've been stalking him ever since." I was shocked he gave her that little information, but I was about to fuck her entire world up.

"Cara, I need to get back. If it's something you want, just say it." She sounded aggravated.

"I want you to make him see, I'm the woman for him." She scoffed up a laugh.

"Cara, I can't make him see anything."

"Sure, you can. Tell him, you have a disease that won't go away and then, send him my way."

"You sound crazy. Cara, he and I, have been intimate many times and he knows, my body is clean. I'm pregnant for God's sake." I sucked my teeth. He did tell me, she's the only woman who he'd run up in, raw.

"Well, figure it out."

"You're crazy." She shook her head in disappointment.

"If you didn't throw yourself at him, he'd be with me."

"You and I, both know that's not true."

11

"Did he ever tell you we fucked?" She stopped walking to the door and stared at me. I could tell, she was trying to figure out if I was lying.

"Yea, right. He wouldn't do that to me, regardless, if we were speaking or not." Now, it was my turn to laugh. I pulled my phone out, found what I was looking for, and pressed play.

"Yes, Marco. Fuck, you feel so good."

"Shut the fuck up. You've wanted this dick, so take it." You heard him say. She covered her mouth.

Of course, Bobbi and I, set it up to record him. When I got to his house that night, we set the phone up and hit record, before he jumped out the shower. We knew she wouldn't believe he fucked me, because he always made it seem like he hated me. He may have caught me with the condom thing, but he missed the camera. Granted, you couldn't really see much because it was dim in the room, but you damn sure heard us.

"How could you do that to me?"

"You're not woman enough for him."

"Why Cara? Why do you want him so bad?"

12

"He needs me and we both know it." She shook her head and let the tears fall.

"You can't be that delusional."

"You have no idea, bitch." I punched her in the face and she stumbled against the wall and fell.

"Oh my God, Cara." Bobbi yelled out. She was about to help her up, but I snatched her away.

"OH NO!" Rakia yelled and I heard how scared she was.

"My water broke. Please get someone in here to help me." I smirked because it was too early for her to deliver.

"I think the bastard baby, needs to die. What you think Bobbi?"

"Cara, this isn't right. We need to get her help."

"If you even think about running your mouth, once we step out this bathroom. Its gonna be a problem." Yea, she was scared to death of me.

"But.-"

"But nothing."

"Cara, please. I'm bleeding and its hurting." She was hysterical crying. I snatched Bobbi's hand and walked out the door. I wish the fuck, I would help her.

"You were in there five minutes too long. Did you tell her?" My mom asked.

"Yup, and she's upset." Is all I said and made my way through the crowd of people.

I made sure not to look at Marco but it was impossible, when I wanted to see my future man. The way I see it, is after my cousin bleeds to death, he'll mourn and I'll be right there to help him through it. Unfortunately, once our eyes met, I knew it would be a problem. He stood up and glanced around the hall. I'm assuming he was looking for Rakia. Tech, must've noticed something too because he was right behind him. Outta nowhere, Rahmel, Ang and my grandfather stood up and their eyes landed on me.

I shrugged my shoulders and went to give my great aunt a hug. Not too long after, I felt an excruciating pain in my arm. I turned around and Marco was coming towards me full speed, with his gun pointed at me. People were screaming and

14

running but he was focused, solely on me. *Why didn't I just*

leave?

Marco

"Where's Rak?" Ang, asked when she came from changing lil man.

"In the bathroom, didn't you see her?"

"The bathroom is right there." She pointed in the opposite direction of where Rakia went.

"She went to the one closer to the back door." Once I said that, my instincts kicked right in. I glanced around the room and my eyes, met Cara's. She came from the direction of the bathroom, but there's no way, she knew my girl was in there.

"What's up?" Tech, stood.

"When did Cara get here?"

"CARA!" Ang, shouted and handed the baby to her mom. Her grandfather was now standing and so was Rahmel. I took off towards the bathroom and so did everyone else. I opened the door and my entire world came crashing down. My girl, was on the floor, with blood seeping through her legs and barely breathing.

"CALL 911!" I shouted and walked out. I took my gun out, found my target and took a shot. I gave zero fucks about this being a repast, or who was in my way. I saw her fall forward and shot again. Her body jerked. The closer I got, the more people screamed and ran. I went to shoot again and Tech, grabbed my arm.

"Another time. Rak, needs you." It took him and a few other people to hold me back, from killing that bitch.

"Where is she?"

"I had the guard put her in the truck and take her to the hospital. The ambulance would've taken too long. Let's go." I grabbed our things from the table and ran out. He was in his truck waiting. I asked where Ang was and he said, with her. At least, someone she knew was there.

He sped to the hospital and I hopped out the truck, just as he put it in park. We ran inside and they were taking her upstairs, to labor and delivery. I told them, I'm the father and I'm going. None of them argued and let me on the elevator. I stared down at her and she could barely keep her eyes open. Her bottom half was full of blood and the tears were rolling

17

down her face. I felt like shit, because I should've been there, but she didn't want me to.

"Sir, I need you to put this on and follow me." One of the nurses said and handed me a gown, a mask and some hair thing. I did what she asked and was on her heels.

"Can you to stand here and keep mommy as calm as possible?"

"What are you about to do?"

"First and ultrasound and if necessary, an emergency C-section."

"But its too early."

"Sir, she's lost a lot of blood, which mean every second that passes, your child is losing air." I nodded and picked up Rakia's hand. They were putting an IV in her arm and monitors on her chest.

"Marco." She said softly.

"Yea, babe. I'm right here."

"Kill her."

"I'm going to." I kissed her lips and wiped her tears.

18

"Ok, we have to do a C-section." Rakia didn't say anything. They wheeled her into another room and started setting things up.

"Here we go. Mommy, you're going to feel some pressure, but you'll be fine." The doctor said and I watched him cut her stomach open. He then cut something else and not too long after, my daughter Brielle Marie Santiago was born, weighing four pounds, three ounces. I shed some tears, watching them pull her from Rakia and hearing her tiny scream. They rushed her to the NICU and closed my girl up.

"We have a daughter ma. She's gonna be as beautiful as you." She smiled.

"I'm tired, Marco."

"Rest your eyes. I'll be right here when you wake up." She didn't respond and closed her eyes. I panicked, thinking she died.

"FUCK!!!! What's going on?" The doctor pushed me out the way.

Once he checked her, he told me the blood loss and medication, made her sleepy. He showed me the screen. Her heartrate, blood pressure and everything else, they monitored, was normal. I was relieved because a nigga would've been lost, if she died.

After they stitched her up, and put her in a room, I hurried to the NICU floor, to check on my daughter. They had her under some light with a tube in her nose. She was breathing fast and I got nervous. Of course, they said, all babies breathe like that and as of right now, she's as perfect as can be. I asked when she could go home and they told me, once she's five pounds and the doctor says its ok. I snapped a few photos, kissed my two fingertips and placed them on the top of her crib.

"No one, and I mean, no one is to come here and see my daughter, unless it's me or her mother. I will sue the fuck outta this hospital, if I find out any one of you let someone up here to see her. Matter of fact, if anyone asks, tell them, there's no one here with the last name Winters. Do I make myself clear?" Every nurse standing there said yes. I told them to leave a note for the other nurses who weren't on shift yet.

"I'll fuck around and kill all you bitches, if anything happens to her. You better act like she's yours, if you value

20

your life." I said on the way out. It didn't matter because the chick in personnel is and old acquaintance and I will let her know, a guard will be here around the clock, until she goes home. I pressed the elevator to go check on my girl. She better be good too, or I'm tearing this hospital up.

****

"Talk to me ma." I said to Rak. She woke up this morning, after the shit from the repast and giving birth. However, she hadn't really said a word.

"What were you going to tell me?"

"Huh?"

"Yesterday, you were supposed to mention whatever my aunt was talking about, when we got home. What was it?" I ran my hand down my face.

"Rak, not right now."

"Yes, right now." She had tears coming down her face, so I knew Cara told her.

"A while back; on my birthday, actually." She stared at me. I was uncomfortable as hell, too.

"The night Bobbi, shouted out the abortion you had, I was mad and went home. She came with me and once we got there, I hopped straight in the shower. Bobbi came in and I told her, I wasn't feeling the threesome she had planned."

"Threesome?" She gave me an aggravated look.

"It was for my birthday Rak. Anyway, I got out the shower and Bobbi and some chick, were already engaged in sex. I couldn't see who she was at first, because the room was dark. I started having sex with Bobbi and the other one, hopped up to suck my dick."

"Ok. Who was the other chick?"

"Rak, I didn't know and when I did, it was too late."

"WHO WAS SHE?" She yelled.

"Cara." I said barely above a whisper.

"Who?"

"Cara, Rak."

"Why Marco? I know, you were free to sleep with anyone but why her? You knew, she was my cousin. The same cousin, who has been doing everything, to get you and she finally got what she wanted." I sat next to her on the bed.

"I'm sorry. It wasn't intentional and I never told you because you had just come home from school, and we weren't together."

"SO WHAT?" She fell back on the bed.

"You're right. It didn't matter that we weren't a couple, but I never wanted to hurt you like that. It was a mistake and had I known it was her, it never would've happened."

"But you did hurt me; the minute you slept with her."

"I knew, I fucked up afterwards; which is why, I kicked her out. The reason, she was beat up and your aunt attacked you, is because she wanted to tell you."

"Well, she told me, alright." She wiped her eyes.

"I figured that." I passed her a tissue.

"What happened in the bathroom?" I asked and she began telling me how Cara and Bobbi, held her in there, spitting lies. The part about us sleeping together, was true but me wanting her and all the other stuff, is straight bullshit. Her cousin is crazy and if she isn't dead yet; she will be.

"Were you ever gonna tell me?" She folded her arms and blew her breath.

23

"Yup, when you married me." I got down on one knee and pulled the ring out my pocket. Last night, after she gave birth and went to sleep. I asked Tech, to pick me up some clothes and bring me the ring, to propose. Him and Ang, knew about the proposal and so did her grandmother. Unfortunately, she passed away and now I'm doing it, with no one around. I did ask one of the nurses to come in and record for me, but it looks like she forgot. Actually, I'm happy no one is here, just in case she says no.

"Maaaarrrco, whhhat are you doinggg." I smiled, listening to her stutter. I took both of her hands in mine, at the same time a nurse walked in. I handed her my phone, hit record and gave it all I had.

"Rakia Winters, you are the love of my life, my soulmate, and my everything. You gave me a daughter and nothing in the world, could top that; except you birthing more of my kids. I love everything about you, from your head, to your pretty ass feet." She chuckled and blushed.

"I know, we've been through a lot and yet, you still stuck around. I respect the shit outta you for that. I love you

24

with every fiber in my body. I want you and only you, to be my wife. Will you marry me?" She was hysterical crying by now. I turned around and there were more nurses and two doctors standing there. Who the hell told them to be nosy?

"I didn't hear you."

"Yes, baby. A thousand times yes." I slid the ring on her finger. She wrapped her arms around my neck and kissed me. I could hear the applause behind me.

"I love you Rak and I promise, we're gonna get through everything together." She nodded and put her hand out to look at the ring.

"Don't you dare ask me how much it cost." She snapped her neck. The ring cost me a hella lot of money. I wanted it to be perfect and for her to be, the only person in the world, with it. The stone alone, cost almost a million dollars. But nothing is too good for her and she's gonna find out, soon.

"I wasn't." She smirked.

"Yes, you were because you're nosy." Her mouth dropped open.

"I love your nosy ass though."

"I love you too." The nurse handed me back the phone and Rak took it, to send the video to herself. She said something about posting the proposal on Instagram. As long as, she said yes, it didn't matter to me, who saw it.

Cara

"I don't wanna see that shit." I told Bobbi. She was on Instagram, watching the video of Marco propose to my retarded ass cousin, for the tenth time.

"Cara, the fucking ring is humongous." I sucked my teeth and rolled my eyes.

I thought for sure, Rakia would've died along with her baby. Unfortunately, I couldn't be lucky. Come to find out, her and the kid survived. My mother tried to see her, but there were two guards on her floor and no one is allowed in there; except him and Rakia. I knew the guards had to be his because of the way, she described them. Only guards that big, work at clubs. Hospitals usually have retired officers and old ass people.

"Bobbi, turn the shit off." I snapped and she put her phone up.

"Can you get me some water?"

"Cara, it's in front of you." I was so distracted, I paid it no mind.

My mom came strolling in, looking like shit. Her eyes had bags under them and her clothes looked worn. I've never seen her in anything less than, expensive. The disheveled look of hers, concerned me. She sat on the chair and let her head fall back. I asked Bobbi to give us a minute and waited for my mom to fill me in. She blew her breath and stared at me.

"Your grandmother had a will."

"She did?"

"Yes. That's where I'm coming from."

"What happened? How much did she leave?" I sat up and got comfortable. My grandmother loved me; regardless of my beef with Rakia.

"She had a million-dollar policy, the house and her car, were in the will, some jewelry and a few other things, I could care less about." I don't understand why she's mad. The million-dollar policy alone, is enough for us.

"Ok, why are you upset?"

"She left Rakia, everything."

"Come again. I don't think, I heard you correctly." My mother had to be playing a joke on me. There's no way my

28

grandmother left Rakia, that kind of money and not me. She would've at least made her three grandkids, split it.

"No, you heard her right." Rahmel strolled in with a grin on his face. He had on Versace clothes, sneakers and glasses. My brother has always done well for himself but this is different. His girl followed behind and it's when I noticed how big her stomach was. Rahmel, never mentioned how many months she was. But by the looks of things, she's ready to pop.

"What are you doing here?" I asked because this hospital is over an hour away and I'm not even sure, how he knew where I was. He came closer to me.

When Marco shot me in the arm and back; my body jerked forward. I remember hitting the floor and that's it. I woke up in this hospital, paralyzed from the waist down and with, a shattered collarbone. My mother told me, Tech grabbed Marco and left to be with Rakia. People came running over to help and since the ambulance was called for my cousin and she left, they took me instead. Thankfully, someone told them to take me elsewhere; otherwise I doubt, I'd be alive. It doesn't take away the fact, he's still going to kill me.

"I came to see how you were. You know since you punched your pregnant cousin in the face and left her to die." I waved him off and he snatched my good wrist and twisted it.

"You are my sister and I love you but the lengths you're going through, to chase a man, who doesn't want you, is pathetic."

"Rahmel, it's hurting."

"Like Rak was hurting, when you sent her into early labor? And you pulled that bullshit the day of grandma's funeral. What the fuck is wrong with you?"

"Rahmel, stop it." He twisted it harder and tossed my arm so hard, I hit myself in the face.

"And you." My mom stared at him.

"You entertaining her ass, like shit is cute. Rakia, loved and looked up to you. One lie from Cara and you flip on her. What? You tryna fuck him too? I mean, you're being as desperate, as she is."

WHAP! My mom smacked the hell outta him.

"OH, HELL NO! Mother or not, I'll beat your ass over this one." Rahmel's girlfriend dropped her purse, yanked my

30

mother by the hair and started punching her in the face. Rahmel, pulled her away and told her to go down into the ER, to be checked. She had to be at least five or six months pregnant, and here she is fighting; his mom at that.

"You'll let this bitch hit your mother?" My mom was holding her nose.

"As of now, I have no mother or sister and don't call her a bitch again."

"Rahmel." He headed for the door.

"I came to say goodbye to you."

"Rahmel, please don't say that. You're my brother." He laughed.

"Marco is going to kill both of you. The way I see it is, I may as well, get used to not seeing you because he's not gonna have mercy on you." He chucked up his two fingers and walked out. My mom ran in the bathroom and turned the water on.

"Ma, do you think he's gonna kill us?"

"Us?" I had to laugh at her.

"I know, you don't think he excluded you." She sucked her teeth.

I put my head on the pillow and closed my eyes. Rakia, was still getting everything she wanted from my grandmother, even in death. On top of that, she had Marco, showering her with gifts, houses, and babies. It's time to figure out, how to get rid of her, once and for all.

I asked my mom to pass me her phone and called Bobbi. I don't know where she went and it was taking her a long time to come back.

"Where are you?"

"In the cafeteria eating. Are y'all finished?"

"Yea. Do me a favor and call Shana. Ask her for Zaire's phone number."

"Zaire?"

"Yes, Zaire. I think it's about time, he and I have a conversation." I hung up and passed the phone to my mother. Hopefully, this plan will work because the other ones, have been falling through.

Tech

"Congratulations, bro. It's about time, y'all got it together." Doc, said to Marco. He proposed to Rak, two weeks ago and the nigga was on cloud nine.

"Thanks. Let me get another drink." The waitress walked away and to the bar.

"You know, you're the best man, right?"

"Man, shut yo drunk ass up."

"I'm serious. There's no one else, I'd rather have in my wedding, standing next to me and my wife, but you and I guess, Ang."

"Bro, don't come for my wife. I'll make sure, to let her know what you said, too."

"Man, ain't nobody stunting Ang." He waved me off and we took the shots, the waitress brought over.

I sat back and allowed some stripper to dance in front of me and he did the same. Oh, we still niggas, but ain't no chick seeing this dick. She started twerking and dropping it, like she was getting fucked. The minute she sat on my lap, I kindly lifted her up. I didn't need her grinding on me too hard and my wife smell it, when I got home. I have enough issues with Shana, and don't need more.

"Come on Tech. Your wife ain't here. Let me have you and Marco."

"We good."

"I won't tell." She continued begging and the shit turned me off.

I don't know what happened with Marco but outta nowhere, he threw the other stripper off his lap and stood up. His drink fell on the floor and he had murder in his eye. I had no clue who he was looking at, until he pointed at Bobbi. He took off down the steps, with me right behind him. This may be my club, but I didn't want him murking her, here.

I know people think, I keep stopping him from killing and they're right. It's a time and place for everything. We may have the police in our back pocket but one video, from a nosy motherfucker, could put us away for life. I'm not saying we'd automatically got to jail but once the feds get involved, it's a little harder to get out of.

"What the fuck you doing here?" He snatched her up and drug her out the side door. She looked scared as hell.

"I told her not to do it, Marco. When she hit her, I tried to help your girl up but Cara threatened me."

"When the fuck did you become scared of anyone?" He pulled his gun out and placed it on her forehead. As long as, he was fucking Bobbi, we've never known her to be worried about another bitch, so hearing she was scared of Cara, threw us for a loop.

"I wasn't, until she tried to kill me, in my sleep."

"WHAT?"

"One night, we had just finished having sex and she was mad, hearing about you getting her cousin pregnant. Anyway, after listening to her bitch and moan, I fell asleep. She must've started drinking because she woke me up. Cara, choked me and put a knife to my throat. She kept yelling, "*I'm gonna kill you Rakia, for taking my man.*" I had to fight her off, and it wasn't an easy task. When she calmed down, I looked at her and its like, she was a different person. Her eyes were red and she was breathing heavy. She may be paralyzed but she is fucking obsessed, with killing Rakia."

"Tha fuck. Where is she?"

"At the hospital, in Atlantic City." He put his hand on the trigger and went to pull it. Bobbi, was hysterical crying.

"Not yet, bro."

"What you mean? She was in the bathroom with Rak. I can't let her live." I moved him away from her.

"Let's see if her story checks out first. If it does, she'll probably be the only one, who could get us close to her. Especially, with your father hiding both of them." I took the gun from him.

"Not right now." He walked over to her.

"I swear, if you're lying, I'll find you and feed you to my pit bull. That way, you'll suffer even more." Yea, this crazy nigga, had a big ass pit bull, he allowed to eat motherfuckers. I tried telling my wife, he's worse than me but she says, were one in the same.

"I'm not lying." I told her to get up and leave. She hauled ass outta there.

"Let me get your ass home to Rak, before you be out here killing everyone."

"Fuck you. Her ass is going to die."

"I know but we need to use her, so keep your trigger finger off the gun for a minute." I understood his frustration, because had this been Ang, I'd be doing the same thing. We never went back in the club. I drove his ass home and had Rak, meet him at the door. Anytime he saw her, a huge smile would come on his face. He was truly in love with her and her feelings, were the same.

"Is he ok?" She asked, when I opened my door.

"Yea. He'll tell you in the morning."

"Come on Rak. I need you right now."

"MARCO!" She blushed. I don't know why she played shy in front of me. Shit, they fuck as much as, Ang and I.

"Tech, don't care. He knows, I'm about to fuck the shit outta you. Or do you wanna do me?" She pushed him in the house. I hope she doesn't get pregnant right away. She did just deliver, two weeks ago and we all know, women are fertile as hell after a pregnancy. I drove to my house, closed the front door and my wife was standing there with a see-through robe and heels on.

I wasted no time, scooping her up and taking her in the room. She turned some music on and had me sit on the bed. I started taking my sneakers off and looked up, to see her dancing for me. Shit, I didn't even know she could twerk, or get down the way she was and I damn sure wasn't complaining. My dick was hard as hell watching her. She lifted her leg on the side and told me not to touch. How the hell did she expect that, when her juices were beginning to seep out her pussy? I leaned back on the bed, let her undo my jeans and slide them off.

"I see my husband wants me."

"Always baby." I let my hands go up and down her legs.

"I'll always want you too." She turned around, sat down and started riding me. Her ass, was smacking against my legs and I couldn't get enough of watching it jiggle. My wife maybe much younger than me, but her bedroom skills are the best, I've ever experienced. Older woman couldn't fuck with her sexually, on her bad day.

"I'm pregnant again." She grabbed my knees and dropped down harder.

"I already knew." She leaned back and went in circles. She could always get me to cum, fast this was.

"Fuck me harder, Tech." I grabbed her waist and pumped harder. Her body was shaking and my nut was at the top.

"Shittttttt. Ang, you're the best, I ever had." I stuck my tongue in her mouth.

"That's cuz, I know what you like. Let me, get you up again."

"We good Ang. Oh shit. Fuck!" She swallowed me and needless to say, we had a long night.

****

"You're about two and half months pregnant. Do you wanna see the baby?" The doctor asked.

"Yup. I need to see if my daughter is in there." Her and Ang, started laughing.

"You do know, we won't find out the sex for a few months?" I sucked my teeth. I wanted to know now. I refused to wait until delivery, like Marco and Rak did. They decided to be surprised and they were. At the time, Rak wanted a boy and he wanted a girl, which he got what he wanted. It's funny how it was the opposite with them. Now he was ready for his son.

"Here is the prescription for the prenatal vitamins and your appointment, in four weeks. I don't have to tell you, the do's and don'ts of being pregnant." We shook our head no and walked out.

"I hope it's a girl. Brielle will have a best friend." She smiled. I opened the car door for her.

"Me too. I need someone else to spoil." She sucked her teeth.

"You better not get jealous already." I leaned in and kissed her.

"I'm not but you better make sure, she doesn't cut in on my sex time. I love doing nasty thing to you." I shut my door and stared, as she licked her lips.

"Oh, yea."

"Do I need to remind you?" I started the car and backed out. I knew where she was going with this and the best thing for me to do, is move out this parking lot.

"I think you do." She took her seatbelt off, pulled my dick out and gave me some of her A1, head game. I almost crashed twice.

"How are you gonna see the baby with my dick on your breath?" She pulled a small bottle of mouthwash out her purse. I shook my head and started laughing. My wife is a trip and always prepared. We parked in the lot and went inside.

****

"What up bro? Where's my niece?" Ang and I, walked in the room. They allowed Marco and Rakia, to stay with her.

"Rak, is feeding her. Why you bring her?" He mushed Ang.

"You got one more time and I'll make sure Rak don't marry your ass."

"Yea right. She love this nigga, too much to diss me. Right ma."

"Your ass will be standing alone at the altar, if that dick even thinks about, getting hard for another woman. I don't care if she's a stripper, it better stay soft." She handed Brielle to Ang, after she put the gown and gloves on.

"Oh shit. I think Rak, has been around us too long. Let me find out she bossing up on you." He pulled her in front of him.

"With that good shit she got, she can boss up anytime she wants."

"That dick pretty good. You can boss up on me too, papi." The smirk on his face told it all. He done turned her geeky ass, into a damn freak.

"On that note, I'll check on my niece." I put the gown and gloves on and sat next to Ang.

"I'm so glad she didn't lose her. Look, how precious she is." Brielle was gorgeous. She was a spitting image of Marco and had a head full of hair. Her eyes were light brown and she was spoiled already. Ang, tried to put her down and she wasn't having it.

We stayed up there for a few hours with them. They stayed most nights, and when they didn't, Lizzie would. Brielle never stayed alone and she never will. With the crazy ass people trying to get Rak, Marco isn't taking any chances. Bad enough, he had the fence people, come to remove the old one and put up a new one. The shit is so high, you can't see in, even if you stood on a car and it went around the entire property.

He updated the security system in and out the house and even had, two bullet proof trucks shipped from overseas. He gave me one to drive but Ang, had it most of the time. Me, I was cool with my old truck, plus I got my own guns to bust back with. Unfortunately, people were trying their hardest to come for us and our girls. It's time to bring out the old us and I can tell you now, it's not gonna be nice.

Angela

"I'll be back babe." I kissed Tech on the lips and he pulled me on top of him.

"Let me get some first."

"Tech, I told Rak, I'd come over to see Brielle. And we had sex all night." I slid my tongue in his mouth.

"Why you playing?" He squeezed my ass and grinded me on top of him. I felt him getting hard and stood up.

"Yea, my wife knows what time it is." I took my clothes off and gave my husband a dose of what he loves the most from me.

"Bring my son home." He smacked me on the ass, when I stepped out the shower.

"You need to talk to your mom. The last time, I went to get him from her, she damn near, cursed me out. Talking about, I'll bring him, when I'm ready and don't bring your ass over here to get him, either." We both busted out laughing. Even though she was Marco's birth mother, you would think, she was his too.

Marco and Tech, have been friends since they were kids and back then, she treated him like her own, along with the other guy, Dennis. They did everything together and when his mom died, she jumped right in to take her place. He said, she's never overstepped boundaries and he'd do anything for her, as well. I actually, loved the relationship between them. Its genuine and had he not told me, she wasn't really his mom, I would've never known.

I grabbed the keys, kissed his cheek and ran out the door, before he pulled me back in the room. Its no secret, my husband and I, have a lot of sex. Shit, we're young and it's what we're supposed to do. I hope when we get older it's the same because the longer you're with someone, things can change and I don't want that. Lord knows, we had our issues already, so at least, that part is outta the way. Our next journey is raising our kids, if we can ever keep them in the house. Our son and pretty soon, Brielle will only know, Lizzie as the one who always has them. Love her to death, but she really spoils the hell outta lil Antoine, and Brielle is next.

I parked in front of the estate and pressed the button on the gate. Marco, had this place like Fort Knox; especially now that Brielle came home yesterday. They kept her for a month to make sure she gained weight. Her lungs were clear and she had no infections. Rakia, called me crying, when the doctor told her she could go home. I thought something happened, until Marco took the phone from her and explained it all. The two of them, have gone through a lot, to stay together. I know he's gonna protect her and that's all I care about.

"Where's my brother?" Marco, questioned when I walked to the door.

"Damn, can I get in first? And, if you must know, I just threw it on him, so he's taking a nap."

"Tha fuck, Ang. I don't wanna hear that shit." He slammed the door and walked off.

"What's wrong?" Rakia asked, coming out the kitchen with Brielle in her arms.

"He's mad because I told him, Tech is taking a nap, since I wore that ass out." She started laughing. I went in the kitchen to wash my hands, so I could hold her.

"She's so pretty. Awwww Bri, Bri." I let my nose rub hers and kissed her cheek. I tried not to kiss her too much, due to her skin being so sensitive. People see newborns and kiss all over them, causing their skin to break out.

I sat over there for a few hours and asked if she wanted to go out to dinner with me and Lizzie. I called and told her, my son was coming home. After she cursed me out, she wanted us to meet her. Marco, came and took Brielle. She cuddled up in his chest and Rakia, sucked her teeth. She said, he's the only one she does that with. I guess, she's a daddy's girl already. She kissed both of them and we left.

Lizzie had us meeting her at some fancy ass restaurant. Not that we couldn't afford to eat there but there was a line and a bitch, is hungry. She met us at the door but my son wasn't with her. Some guy came out and ushered us in. When I asked where lil Antoine was, she said, Tech came and snatched him up, before she left. I laughed, because we both missed him and planned on keeping her and my parents away for a few days. Well, we're gonna try because they all have a key to the house. Knowing them, they'll take him in the night.

"What can I get you ladies?" We gave the waitress our drink and appetizer orders. She walked away and Rakia looked stressed out.

"What's wrong?" I asked and continued looking at the menu.

"Nothing." She pouted and we both looked at her.

"Rakia, spill it." Lizzie accepted her glass from the waitress and so did Rak. She handed me, my soda.

"Ok, so. I wanna have a big wedding, with the limo ride to the church, the bachelorette party, and everything. You know the whole Cinderella theme."

"What's the problem?"

"I don't have anyone to be there. You two are my only friends, my grandmother passed, two of my family members, want me dead and I think Marco got me pregnant again." She busted out crying and we fell out laughing.

"Well, first of all… you two horn dogs, should've strapped up or waited for birth control to kick in." Rakia looked at Lizzie.

"Your ass didn't get on any, did you?" She shook her head no.

"Anyway, who cares, if you're pregnant again?"

"I do. I wanted Brielle, to be at least two before we had another one."

"All, I can tell you is, if you are, you better have the doctor, put you on birth control before he stitch yo ass up, after you deliver this one." She had a grin on her face.

"Second… Honey, Marco has a huge family and trust me, they're all waiting to meet you."

"Me?" The lady handed us the appetizers and took down the rest of our order.

"Yes, you. The woman, who got him to settle down. The one, who took him away from Mia."

"I didn't take him." Lizzie and I, both stared at her. Is she serious? She may not have been around when they dated, but we all knew how deep his feelings ran for Mia. Well, I knew from Tech.

When she came to town, Tech told me, he was gonna fuck up. I couldn't tell Rak, because I wanted to give him the benefit of the doubt. Unfortunately, once he saw her, supposedly, she let the fake ass tears fall and he got caught up. I understand, why he felt the need for closure but he didn't have to sleep with her, to get it. I guess, he knew too because Rak, gave him her ass to kiss, in order to take him back. I don't think if he almost killed Mia, she would have, just yet. She really let him know, just because she wasn't as experienced as other woman, cheating is cheating and he had to be taught a lesson.

Tech, told me he was stressing like crazy without her. I said, that's what he gets. Now, he barely wants her outta his sight and tried twice, to go finish Mia off but Rak, stopped him. She said, it was enough and her son didn't deserve to lose both parents. Sheiiittttt, a bitch like me, would go right with my man and take pictures. I need a reminder, fuck that.

"Hello." We looked up and it was Shana. Now, this is a bitch, who deserved a knife in the chest. She tries me every time she sees me. I promised Tech, I wouldn't touch her but she makes it very hard.

"Hello. And you are?" Lizzie asked. She was gangsta as hell.

"I'm Shana. Tech's mistress." I went to stand up but Rak, put her hand on mine.

"I'm sorry but my son doesn't have mistresses, side chicks, or ho's. You must be mistaken."

"Oh, you're his mom. He told me all about you. I must say, you have two handsome sons." I opened and closed my fists, to keep calm.

"What did you say your name was again?" Lizzie wiped her mouth and waited for her to answer.

"Shana. I used to work at his club, until his wife began acting like a baby, because she caught us coming out his office." Lizzie stood up.

"Oh, now I remember. I think Tech, did mention you." She had a smirk on her face.

"You're the bitch, who came in his office unannounced and let him cum in your mouth." Shana's mouth fell open.

"The one, who thought she could take him from my daughter in law, Ang."

51

"They weren't married at the time and he obviously, wasn't happy, if I could get him." I thought about what she said, and wondered if he was happy back then? How could he be, if he cheated?

"Honey, let me school you real quick." She moved closer to Shana and Rakia, stared at me.

"A man, has a dick that gets hard, at the sight of most women." Lizzie looked Shana, up and down.

"I have to say, you're pretty and by the way your clothes are painted on, I'm sure you have a nice body, but let me ask you this." Shana folded her arms.

"You had oral sex with a man, you knew was involved with another woman, thinking he would leave her for you? How'd did it work out for you?" Shana couldn't say shit.

"The problem with women, who sleep with taken men, have low self-esteem and other insecurities going on. It's the reason they become side chicks, and mistresses. Trying to take someone else's man, has become a task for women these days but honey, let me be the first to tell you. Whether my son made

52

you his mistress or not, he's never gonna leave Ang, as I'm sure you can tell and you know why?"

"Why?"

"No man, will ever give up his soulmate, for side pussy. Maybe one day, you'll get to experience true love but until then, stop trying to destroy everyone else's, happily ever after. Now get the fuck out my face, before I allow Ang, to beat that ass like she wants to."

"Yea right. That bitch, can't beat me." I stood up.

"Well, today's your lucky day."

"ANG, NO!" Rakia yelled out but it was too late. I punched her in the face and kept hitting her.

"That's enough." Lizzie and Rak, stood there as some guy pulled me off.

"Like I said, don't bring your ass around her again because she won't be the one, beating your ass. Get her the hell outta here."

"IT'S ON ANG!" She screamed going out. People were staring.

53

"RAKIA, ZAIRE IS COMING FOR YOU AND I HOPE HE KILLS BOTH OF YOU!" The bitch yelled out and I could see fear all over Rakia's face.

"Don't even think about getting nervous." Lizzie said and sat down.

"But?-"

"But nothing. Marco, isn't going to let anyone hurt you." She nodded and asked if I was ok. Tech, was gonna kill me.

"I'm surprised we didn't get kicked out." Rakia said and lifted her fork to eat.

"How can we get kicked out of your restaurant?"

"Huh?"

"Ugh, the name on the place says, Rakia's Fine Cuisine." She ran out to the front and looked up. Lizzie gave us an address to the place and not the name. Neither of us paid attention to the sign coming in because we were more worried about the line. She came in and sat down.

"But when? How?"

"Honey, Marco has been building this place, for a while now. He was gonna name it after him but once you came in his life, he's done a lot of things differently. You have no idea, the number of things you own, do you?"

"WHAT?" She was shocked.

"Look, you two have to speak with your men. They may not have informed you but they don't live legally and want to make sure, if anything ever happened to them, you would be set." I smiled because Tech, told me some of the stuff he put in my name. I guess, Marco forgot or was waiting, to tell her later.

"I don't have anything to buy for him." I made her look at me.

"Rak, you and his children, are the only things he wants from you."

"I know but these things cost money." She waved her hand around the place.

"Rak, some of the best things in life, to a person are free. You birthed his daughter and will have all his kids. He's about to give you everything because there's nothing, he could

55

ever do, to repay you for it. Enjoy this life you're about to receive." She smiled and put her head down.

We stayed in her restaurant a little longer. Lizzie was a little tipsy, so we made her leave the car she drove and I took her home. I dropped Rak off and told her, we could discuss the wedding tomorrow. I pulled out the driveway and drove home. It didn't take me long to get there, since we only lived a few streets over. Before anyone assumes we did this, we didn't. The two of them, already had these houses built from the ground up. I also, loved the fact, no other bitch has ever been in here. I opened the door and my husband was standing there with my son, looking like a damn snack.

"I'm not mad, because she was owed the ass whooping but don't put your hands on her or anyone else again. It's my job to handle her. My wife, is not going to be out there, fighting and being ghetto." Lizzie called him on the phone while we were eating. I expected him to ask, to speak to me but he didn't. I guess, he was waiting for me to get here.

"Ok." He came closer and lifted my face.

"I love you Ang and I'm glad you didn't entertain the shit she said."

"Are you happy with me Tech?"

"As happy as I could ever be. I know, she probably brought up me cheating because Shana's petty like that. Just know, your bedroom skills are nothing to fuck with. I made a mistake and it had nothing to do with not being happy." I nodded.

"Do I need to put him to sleep and show you why you're the best and how happy, I am?" I smiled.

"I'll be in the room, after I put him to bed." I walked up the steps.

"And don't think, I'm not beating the pussy up."

"Tech."

"You still had no business fighting with my daughter in your stomach." I stomped up the steps and slammed the door. After I got out the shower, he was waiting for me and did exactly what he said, he would. My ass was so sore, I laid in the bed the entire next day but it was surely worth it.

Rakia

"So, I see you're out here alone." My aunt Shanta said. I was at the grocery store, getting food for the week. Marco, wanted pulled pork and a bunch of other things. I loved cooking for him.

"What do you want?" I reached in the meat section, for the pork. She walked to the front of the cart and looked at Brielle.

"Oh my God, Rakia. She's beautiful." I smiled but when she reached in, to take her out, I had to shut it down. She may be my aunt but I don't trust her.

"I can't hold her?"

"HELL NO, BITCH. ARE YOU CRAZY? BACK THE FUCK UP BEFORE I LAY YOUR ASS OUT, IN THIS STORE." Marco yelled coming from around the corner. He went to grab some other things he wanted, right before she came around. Her facial expression was funny because she assumed, I was alone.

"Why are you still with him? You know he slept with Cara." He popped her upside the head a few times, like she was a kid. I couldn't do anything but laugh.

"She knows everything, so you blasting it, isn't gonna make her leave me."

"You're gonna let him hit me?"

"He didn't hurt you Shanta and what my fiancé does to people trying to hurt me, is a choice, I agree with. Now, what do you want?" I pushed the cart and Marco started walking with me.

"So, you fuck after your cousin. You're a nasty ho, just like your mother." I stopped in my tracks and turned around.

"Rak." I could hear him calling me but all I saw was red. I smacked my aunt extremely hard in the face. How dare her speak about my mother? She may be on drugs and not able to raise me, but it doesn't give her or anyone else the right, to speak bad about her.

"You fucking bitch." She was about to charge me.

CLICK! I heard and Marco had his gun on Shanta's forehead.

"You got one time, to lay hands on her and they'll be selling your body parts in this store, for $1.99 a pound." I smirked and looked around to make sure no one was looking. The store wasn't crowded but there were some stragglers. People weren't paying us any mind.

"I can't wait until Zaire, kills her." He yanked her by the head.

"Tell that nigga to come outta hiding. It's me he wants and I've been waiting." He slammed her on the floor.

"Oh, and if anything happens to my girl, your father is burying you next." He put the gun in his waist.

"Shit, you need to be thanking Rak."

"For what?" She got up off the floor.

"She's the reason, you're not dead; yet." Shanta looked at me and I rolled my eyes. I know Marco's been waiting patiently, to kill all of them and if it had not been for me, asking him not to, her and Cara, would've been gone.

"I'm sorry, Rakia." I heard, turned around and walked towards her.

"I may be naïve to the streets, but I'm not naïve to someone apologizing to save their life. I gave you chance after chance, to change and you didn't. Whatever my fiancé does from here on out to you and Cara, I'm fine with. I'm done trying to save people, who don't want saving."

"Rak, I thought."

"I don't care what you thought, Shanta. I am your niece. You watched all that I've gone through with Cara and still believed what she told you. Don't say it's because she was your daughter, either. Everyone knew the type of person she was, which is why, you used to get in her ass over it. Marco, came into my life and she wanted him, like she wanted everything I had. She thought, I'd turn him over to her but there's no way, I'd give him up." I saw Marco smiling out the corner of my eye.

"He is one of the few, who's had my back throughout everything. And yes, we had issues but they came from your jealous ass daughter. Shanta, when I walk away, forget you knew me. I no longer exist to you and vice versa." I left her standing there with her mouth hanging open.

Being with Marco, has really given me a voice. I would've never spoken to her like that, any other time. I guess him and Tech, are right about me coming into myself and not allowing anyone to treat me like shit anymore.

"I'm proud of you baby." He held my hand and we finished shopping like nothing happened. Inside, I was smiling because it felt good to say those things to her, without worrying, that she'd lay hands on me.

"Thank you for helping me find my voice."

"It's always been there Rak. You just had to be comfortable in using it." He stopped me from pushing the cart and pulled me in for a kiss.

"I will always have your back, right or wrong."

"Do you crave me yet?" I wiped my lipstick off his lips.

"It's worse, now that you're home."

"Why?"

"Because I never want you to leave my sight. It's like having a favorite blanket, you wanna take everywhere. When you leave it home, the craving for it, gets bad, until you get

62

back to it. You are my favorite blanket Rak, and that's some real shit."

"DAMN! I want a man like him. Do you have any brothers?" Some chick said and we both started laughing.

"He has one, who's married and as you can see, this one is all mine."

"Well damn, I'll take a cousin, uncle or something. A man like him, had to get it from somewhere." She grinned and walked away.

"I crave you too babe. I crave for your touch, your kiss and just being next to you."

"I need to get home and fill your craving, then." I smiled. He kissed my neck and told me to hurry up and finish.

I loved this man with everything I had and even though we had some problems; he shows me every day, I made the right choice in giving him one last chance. And I say one, because he knows, if it happens again, that's it. Nothing he says, will get me to come home.

****

"What are we doing for your twenty first birthday?"
Ang asked and took Brielle out the crib. She had come over
with lil Antoine. She claimed to be hiding him from her parents
and Tech's mom. They've been kidnapping both kids.

"I don't know. I was thinking about a quiet, romantic
dinner with my fiancé and letting him have me, screaming and
moaning, all night."

"Sounds like a plan to me." He kissed the back of my
neck and wrapped his hands around my waist.

"Marco, tell her we should party."

"Hell no. If she only wants to be with me, why you
hating?" The two of them, always went back and forth. Tech,
and I, always get a kick outta them.

"Never hating bro. My man be having me climb walls
too, and.-"

"I'm out yo. I hate when she starts talking that shit."
Ang and I, started laughing. He hated to hear her speak about
the way Tech handled her.

"Ok. I'll see you later."

"Be naked, when I get home."

"Maybe." I bit down on my lip.

"You play too much."

"That's because mami, needs papi, to do some nasty things to her body. You don't wanna hear me moaning your name because, I damn sure wanna say it." He grabbed my hand and Ang slammed, Brielle's door. I heard the television go up.

"Take those fucking clothes off." He locked the door.

"Maybe we should wait. You know.-" He slammed me against the door and literally ripped my t-shirt and shorts off.

"What I tell you about wearing panties in the house? Huh?" He bit down on my shoulder and slid them down my legs.

"I forgot."

"Oh, you forgot." I heard his jeans being unzipped and the anticipation of him entering, was killing me.

"Turn around."

"I think we should wait." He swung me around, placed both of my hands above my head on the door and opened my legs with his.

"Can I do all the things you want me to?" He whispered in my ear, making my body hotter.

"Yesssssss." I moaned out.

"Nah, you know what I wanna hear." His lips were on my neck and his fingers, were in my treasure.

"Papi, I need to feel you." I started speaking Spanish and he plunged inside of me, forcefully but it felt so damn good.

"Fuck me back, Rak." My ass pushed him back some, so I could get comfortable. I placed my hands on the door and had him calling out my name.

"Got damn, Rak. Shit, this pussy is gonna be the death of me. Fuck, you feel so good." He pumped harder and I threw it back faster. I felt him stiffen up and hopped off.

"Yoooooo. Rakia, shittttttt." He shouted, when I placed him in my mouth to catch his seeds.

"You never cease to amaze me, ma. Fuck, I love you." I mounted myself on top and waited for him to get hard, again.

"You're fucking the hell outta me." He smacked me on the ass and the two of us, continued moaning each other's name.

****

"Marco, I don't think, I can walk." I laid in the bed and wanted to go to sleep.

"That's your fault for riding this horse all wild and shit." I smacked his arm.

"Come on." He lifted me up and we showered together.

By the time, we came out the room, I could smell food cooking. We went downstairs and Ang was in the kitchen with Tech and the kids. They both looked at us and started laughing.

"Its about damn time. Bro, we were supposed to be gone an hour ago."

"Its Rak's fault." My mouth dropped open.

"You wanted this dick real bad, mami. Remember, Papi needed to handle you." He whispered in my ear and my face had to turn beet red.

"What you cook?" I went over to the stove and saw fried fish, corn on the cob, and brown rice. She was pulling the last bit of fish out. We all made a plate, sat at the table eating and making jokes. I may not have a lot of friends but these three, were all I needed.

After we all ate, the guys left. Ang and I, bathed the kids and watched some kids' movie, until they went to sleep. Around midnight, she went in one of the spare rooms and I went in my room. I laid there watching television and soon as I was about to dose off, Marco came in. He stripped, showered and got in bed. I put my head on his chest and went straight to sleep.

Marco

I rolled over and noticed Rak, wasn't in the bed but Brielle was. I stared down at her and smiled. My daughter was a replica of me and Rakia, was pregnant again. She tried to tell me, but I cut her off. Shit, I know the change in her pussy, so it wasn't hard to tell. At first, she cried because she wanted to wait for our daughter to get a little older. However, my soldiers wanted a warm spot and knew, if they found her egg, it would be the place to be. It didn't matter to me, if she was barefoot and pregnant, every year. Money wasn't an issue and like most men say, no other woman will bare my kids. Bobbi, tried to pull the bullshit but she and I both knew, it was a lie. Sleeping with Rakia, the first time with no protection, actually shocked me. I guess, once she mentioned her virgin status, it was a wrap.

I stood up, put some pillows around Brielle and ran in the bathroom, to wash my face and brush my teeth. I checked on her again and she was still knocked out. Rak, must've fed, changed and put her back to sleep. I turned the shower on and hurried to wash and get out, in case she did wake up. I hated to rush, but I didn't know where Rak was and I couldn't take the chance of her waking up and trying to roll over.

I stepped out, dried off and got myself together. I picked Brielle up and noticed my phone going off. It was a text message from Bobbi, asking if I could meet her somewhere. I had to text Tech, to come with me. It was a possibility, I'd kill her and he said we should keep her ass alive. I told her where to meet me and at what time. Rak, wasn't gonna be happy but if she was assisting in getting Cara, she had to deal with it.

"Damn bae. It smells good as hell down here." I walked up on her and kissed the side of her neck. Brielle's greedy ass woke right up.

"You hungry?" I looked at the eggs, bacon, pancakes, grits, toast and fresh fruit.

"Hell yea." She made my plate, along with hers and sat across from me. The look on her face, told me something was up. I sat my daughter in the vibrating seat and told Rak, to sit next to me. We started eating and she kept staring at me. I cut

70

up some pancakes, put them on my fork and shoved them in my mouth.

"What's up?"

"Marco, you know I love you right?" I dropped my fork. When people say shit like that, it means, something else is gonna come out, you don't wanna hear.

"Don't get upset." I sat back and waited for her to speak.

"Zaire, called me and.-"

"When?"

"Yesterday."

"YESTERDAY!" I shouted and she jumped.

"Rak, why didn't you tell me?"

"You came in late and I didn't wanna bother you." I stood up and tossed the cloth napkin on the table. She didn't like using the paper ones.

"Stop the, "*I don't wanna bother you shit*," Rak. You know, this nigga is tryna get at you and instead of telling me, you continue holding shit in."

"Marco, I'm sorry. Its just.-"

71

"Its just what? You want him or something?"

"What? No. I don't want you to kill anyone else, for me. I mean, definitely get rid of Cara but I don't want anyone else to die."

"Listen to yourself, Rak. This nigga has people telling you, he has plans on killing you. Are you ready to die? Because if I don't get him first, he's gonna take you away from me and Brielle. What about my kid in your stomach?" She put her head down.

"Do you think any of them are worried about me, if you die? You think, they're sitting at home saying, let's not kill him because it'll hurt Rakia? No! They want you dead, to hurt me and vice versa. WHAT THE FUCK RAK?" I was pissed at this point. I walked out the kitchen and she came behind me.

"He said, if you stop coming after him, he won't kill me." I stopped in my tracks and turned around. The look on my face must've been scary because she backed up.

"You had a conversation with him?"

"It was only for a few minutes." I chuckled.

"A few minutes, huh?" I walked up closer to her.

72

"So, I can converse with Bobbi and Mia? You'd be ok with that?" Her face had a frown on it. Not that Mia could speak at the moment, but I was making a point.

"Marco."

"Marco, my ass. I did some foul shit in the past and we moved past it. But one thing for sure is, I would never disrespect you, and converse with a bitch, who wanted you dead."

"Didn't you speak to Bobbi?"

"She was at the club Rak. I tried to kill her but Tech asked me not to, because she's the only one, who knew where your cousin was. We were going to use her to get Cara, and you know this so don't try and use it against me." It wasn't shit she could say.

"I don't hide anything from you, and I've never lied; regardless, of how it would hurt. I've always been straight with you, from day one. And you hiding phone conversations with a nigga who wants both of us dead. You need to think about what you're asking me to do."

"Marco, I don't know what to do anymore. I'm trying to save myself from dying and keep him away from you."

"One thing you never have to worry about, is me being safe. I'll always make it back home to my family. But you, you're on some other shit and right now, I can't be around you. I'm out yo."

"So, what you're running to Bobbi?" *How the fuck did she know about the text? Not that I'm hiding it, but I didn't get the chance to tell her yet.*

"You don't get it, Rak. I gave up everything and everyone for you. I don't want no other bitch or bitches. When I said, you are it, for me; I meant it. I gave you a ring and asked you to take my last name. No other bitch on this planet could ever tell you, I did the same for them."

"I'm sorry, Marco. I was trying to make it easy on everyone and end the feud but I guess, I'm wrong." She went to walk away and I grabbed her arm.

"You were dead wrong!" She had an aggravated look on her face. I guess she thought, I would say something else, like its ok. Hell no, it wasn't because she had no business entertaining the nigga.

"You had no reason to answer his call, or agree to anything. Regardless of what he told you, its basically, whoever he gets first. That nigga, don't mean shit he said to you, but you're so damn naïve, you believed him." I could see she was surprised, I called her that. It wasn't to be disrespectful but she had to know.

"Rak, you're far from stupid so don't make a face, like it's what I called you. What I'm saying is, he knows how forgiven you are and using it against you. Instead of you realizing it, you fell for his bullshit."

"Can't you think about it?"

"Did you hear anything, I said?" She stared at me.

"I can't do this with you right now."

"You're just gonna leave?" I ran up on her.

"You damn right, I am because my fiancé wants me to save her fucking ex. She wants me not to kill him for whatever reason and a nigga, ain't feeling it. Do you remember the shit he did to you?"

"All I'm saying is.-"

"And all I hear is, spare him for me. Fuck outta here with that Rak." I walked to the door and she ran over to me.

"Please don't cheat on me." I stepped back and stared at her.

"Are you serious?" She put her head down and I lifted it up, to see a few tears rolling down her face.

"If you believe, I'd sleep with another woman over an argument, then you obviously don't trust me. And ma, I can't be with anyone who's not secure in her spot." I stepped out the front door.

"Rak, I think we need to take a break."

"What?"

"You don't trust me and you're trying to get me, to save your ex. A man, who will kill me or you, if he comes into contact with us."

"Marco, I don't want space. Please don't leave."

"You think, I'm gonna cheat ma. The way I see it is, every time, I leave this house you feel that way and it don't sit right with me. I'll be by to see my daughter but we need time apart. You need to rethink who's more important to you and if this is, what you really want." I walked to my car and turned around to see her wiping her eyes.

"This is your house, so don't think, I'm kicking you out. I'll see you whenever." I sat down in my car and lit a blunt. I loved the fuck outta Rak, but if she has insecurities about me, we ain't gonna work.

"MARCO!" I heard her scream and pulled off. If I stayed any longer, I'd probably get out and go to her. She had to learn, not everyone has her best interest at heart. Zaire, Cara and everyone else, will be dead soon, whether she agreed or not. I'm not about to allow any of them to roam this earth freely, knowing Rak and my kids are a constant target. Rakia, had me fucked, all the way up.

****

"What the fuck you want?" I asked Bobbi in the office at the club. Tech and I, thought this would be the best place to meet her.

"Cara, is making plans with Zaire, to kill Rak." I shook my head. This is exactly why, I told her, he had a motive for contacting her.

"What's the plan?"

"I don't know yet. She said, since she can't walk, he'll have to figure out how to do it,"

"How the fuck do they know one another and where is he staying?"

"He was staying with Shana at first, then I don't know where he went." Tech looked at me.

"Shana somehow found Cara's number and called her up. Don't ask me how she found out they were related. I can only assume, Zaire told her."

"Where's Cara now?"

"She was at the house this morning, but I called right before coming here and she claimed, her mom came to pick her up. She said, she'd be staying with her from now on, so its no telling where she's at."

"Alright, yo. Thanks for telling me." I stood up and Tech, went in the bathroom. She stood by the window, looking down at the club. No one was in there but the view is nice.

"Marco, do you think, we could still mess around on the side?" I thought the bitch was crazy before, but I know for a fact, she is now. She came walking towards me.

"What the fuck, Bobbi?" I asked when she stuffed her hands in my sweats and pulled my dick out. I grabbed her wrist at the same time, Tech's office door opened.

"Marco?" I froze. Bobbi had a smirk on her face. Did she know Rak was here? I tossed her stupid ass to the ground.

"Rak, I swear, its not what it looks like." Ang, was shaking her head.

"Umm, was your dick in her hand. How did she even get it out?" I had just put it back in but she must've saw me.

"Its because he let me. You should know, not to ever let your man out the house in sweats. Its easy access for the next bitch to pull it out."

"Get the fuck out, yo."

79

"As long as, I got to see and touch it, I'll be able to fantasize about it for a week or two. Thanks baby." She pulled me by the neck and kissed my lips.

"BITCH! ARE YOU FUCKING CRAZY?" I yelled and she ran out the office. I told security to get her and I'll be at the warehouse soon. This bitch, thought shit was funny and I'm done sparing her.

"Marco, I asked you not to cheat on me and this is why?" I thought about trying to defend myself but she's gonna think what she wants. I grabbed my keys and headed to the door. Tech, came out the bathroom, looking confused.

"So, you're just gonna leave and not even.-"

"Not even what, Rak? Huh?" I moved closer to her.

"You want me to say, I fucked her because you made me mad? Nah, I can't. I wasn't thinking about another bitch."

"But she had.-"

"She did have my dick in her hands but you also heard her say, how she was able to do it. I didn't fuck her or had no idea, she'd do that. Then, you saw her kiss me unexpectedly but you're gonna believe what you want." I walked towards the door.

"This is the exact reason, I told you we needed space. You don't trust me."

"I do Marco but what am I supposed to say, walking in on that?"

"You're supposed to ask your man, what's going on and believe he wouldn't do no disrespectful shit to you. Rak, why are you here, anyway? Huh? I made it clear, we needed time apart. Did you come here thinking I was fucking around?" When she put her head down, all I could do was shake mine.

"Tech, hit me up, when you're done here. I'm out." I slammed the door and went to my car. The sooner, I get rid of these motherfuckers, the better off, I'll be. Maybe then, she and I, can get on the right track. Because this back and forth, ain't for me.

Tech

"Yo, what the fuck happened?" I tossed the paper towel in the trash. I saw Ang's face and looked at Rakia, who sat on the couch.

"Bobbi, had Marco's dick in his hands and then kissed him."

"She was leaving when I went to the bathroom. She must've done it, and he wasn't paying attention. Why you sitting over there mad?" Rakia, looked up at me.

"I know, you don't think, he let her do it." Marco already told me, what went down this morning at his house. I had to agree with him, about her being naïve. I would've been pissed too, hearing she spoke to an ex and then, tried to get her man, not to kill him. I know she's naïve and gullible but she can't be that stupid.

"Why was she here?" I turned to look at her.

"Let me school you on my brother, Rak." I sat next to her.

"We all know, he messed up with the Mia shit but one thing he's not, is a cheater." She looked at me.

"Again, he messed up but you need to take blame in it too."

"What?"

"You kept shit from Marco, told him to leave you alone and expected him to stay around, without saying, you still wanted to be with him. The minute you were confident in wanting him, regardless, of how he made you come to your decision, he hasn't even thought about another bitch. All he talks about is you and Brielle. Then today, you ask him to save your ex."

"WHAT?" Ang shouted out. Obviously, she hadn't told my wife.

"Rak, he's in love with you, however, he's not gonna continue letting you play these games. Its either you're in the relationship 100 percent, or not."

"I'm in love with him too."

"Then, I suggest you work harder at proving it. Every time, the two of you get it right, something happens and you start accusing him of wanting others."

"I don't know how to prove it." I grabbed my keys and phone.

"You better figure it out, because he will leave and never come back." I walked over to Ang.

"Let me go get this nigga before he kills everything moving. I'll see you in a few." I kissed her and looked at Rakia, who had tears coming down her face. I couldn't feel bad for her anymore. It's like she was doing dumb shit on purpose and if I'm over it, I know my brother is.

I drove to the warehouse and he was standing outside his car, smoking. I stepped out and stood next to him. I could tell he was stressing. He passed me the blunt and we stood there in silence. This is how we both dealt with shit, while others may act out. I blew smoke out and passed it back.

"I'm trying to understand her bro but I can't. I'm about to say fuck it, and let her go."

"You have to give her another chance." I didn't want them to break up. The love they shared, was Not Your Ordinary, Hood Kinda Love and more like a fairytale, when it came to her. He rescued her from the shit with her family, gave her whatever she wanted and made sure no one fucked with her, if he could help it. To hear him say, he's ready to throw it all away, seemed crazy. Especially, when I know how much they love one another.

"I should because of the chances she gave me. She's not secure in her spot and it's my fault. I fucked up bro, I know. But I'm not about to live the rest of my life, dealing with her thinking, I'm cheating once I walk out the door. What's gonna happen, when we go out of town, or the country and can't take them? If she can't move past it, then she needs to say it. I'm done, with tryna prove it won't happen again."

I understood where he was coming from. I'm glad Ang, didn't act the same way after the shit, with Shana. I definitely learned my lesson and he did too. But who wants to live like that? Rakia, can say she's over it all she wants but her actions are showing different. Why would she come to the club

85

anyway? I'm not saying she can't come but did she automatically think he came there to cheat? Like I told her, he doesn't want anyone but her and she better figure out if she wants only him because once he's fed up, it won't be a thing she can do about it.

"Let's handle this and have some drinks." We walked in the warehouse and Bobbi was sitting in the chair, crying her eyes out.

"I'm sorry Marco. I should've never.-"

PHEW! PHEW! She was dead before finishing her sentence.

****

"Is he ok?" Ang asked, when Marco and I, came in the house. It was after two in the morning but he was too drunk to drive home.

"Yea. He didn't wanna go home." I closed the door and went down the hall with her.

"Baby, I didn't know she asked him that." I started taking my clothes off.

"I could tell by your expression."

"I don't know what's wrong with her, or why she even thought to ask some shit like that." I pulled her in the shower with me. She whined because her pajamas got wet. I took them off and pushed her against the wall. Sex with my wife is always mind blowing and a nigga happy as hell, she never put up a fight.

"If you ever ask me to do some shit like that, I'll kill you." I said as we laid in the bed.

"I would never."

"Does she love him or something?"

"I asked her the same thing Tech, and to be honest, she doesn't want anything to do with him. She blocked his phone number, after we left the club. I really think, she believes everything will go back to normal, if Marco doesn't kill him. She has no idea, Zaire is using her. I wanna say she's not that stupid, but asking him to do this type of shit, makes me think she may be a tad bit ditzy."

"She doesn't understand the ramifications of having a hit out on her." Ang, sat up and looked at me.

"I mean, she's so use, to forgiving people for yelling at her, being mean, talking about her and trying to hurt her, that she's immune to it. Babe, it's the only thing she knows how to do. She doesn't realize, her forgiving them doesn't mean, they'll let bygones, be bygones." She sat on my lap.

"Baby, she really is, in love with Marco."

"I know she is." I grinded her bottom half on my dick. She and I, could fuck all night and still fuck again in the morning.

"I don't want him to leave her."

"He's trying not to, Ang. But I think, she pushed him away asking that." She nodded and started sucking on my neck.

"I guess, she'll have to figure it out."

"Yup." I lifted her up and slid her down.

"Take care of your husband again."

"Anything for you. Sssssss. I love this dick." I smiled and watched as she let her head fall back to ride me. My wife was beautiful and her sex faces, always made me cum harder.

After we finished, we went to bed, only to be woken up, a short time later by Ang's phone ringing off the hook. I looked and it was Rakia. Why the hell is she calling at four in the morning? I picked it up and she was crying. I asked what happened and she claimed Zaire, called and said he was gonna kill her grandfather, if she didn't meet him somewhere. This nigga was really getting on my nerves. I took the phone in the room with Marco and he was passed out.

"Rak. Marco, is knocked out. Are the alarms on, in the house and on the gate?"

"Yea."

"You'll be fine. He can't get in and I doubt, he even knows where you live. Your grandfather will be fine. He's been staying with Rahmel." I thought she knew but I guess not.

"Ok."

"I'll have him call you, when he gets up." She said ok and hung up.

"That nigga, called and threatened her, didn't he?" Marco asked and turned over. I thought he was passed out.

"Yup."

"Maybe, she'll see shit for what it really is."

"What you gonna do?" I sat on the edge of the bed.

"Nothing. She's safe on the estate and when she leaves, someone will continue watching her. I can't deal with the bullshit right now."

"And him?"

"He'll show his face eventually." I stood up to leave.

"Yo, you think he's at Shana's?"

"I didn't even think to go there. We'll hit her up tomorrow. I'm sure, she'll love to hear from me." I smirked. Marco had crazy ass Bobbi, Cara and Mia, while I had, crazy ass Shana. I'm sure, she won't have an issue, opening the door for me. Little does she know, it won't be for what she wants.

Angela

"So, are you gonna leave her?" I asked Marco, when he came walking in the kitchen.

"It's too early Ang, damn. Can I eat?" He mushed me in the head, like always and took lil Antoine, from me.

"She already called here twice for you." I could see him smile.

"Are you gonna make me a plate?"

"Nigga, I ain't your wife."

"No, but you're her best friend. You wouldn't want me to tell her you didn't feed me, and had me starving, while you and Tech, ate a big ass breakfast."

"She wouldn't believe you." He gave me this look.

"You're right, she would but I still ain't making your plate." I sat down to eat next to my husband and this nigga, took my plate. Tech, busted out laughing and guess what? I took his. I bet, he wasn't laughing no more.

"Alright Ang. You wanna play. Don't say nothing, when I'm eating the shit out that pussy and you begging me to stop." I heard a loud noise. Marco dropped his fork and turned his face up.

"I lost my fucking appetite."

"Nigga please. All the shit talking you and Rak, do. Eat your damn food, so we can go." He sucked his teeth and took his plate in the living room.

"That's what his ass gets." I said and got up to make Tech, another plate. By the time, I finished, he was done with mine.

"I'm out baby. Thanks for breakfast."

"Tech, be careful." I knew he was going to Shana's, to see if she'd tell them where Zaire was. I had no worries at all. It took me a minute to trust him again but I had full faith in him, not to hurt me. Plus, he knows, I'll go fuck someone else to piss him off. And whether he kills me afterwards, it won't matter because someone will have, had me and he doesn't want that.

"Always." He kissed me and brought our son to me.

I cleaned up after they left and got my son dressed to leave with Lizzie. She hadn't seen him in two weeks because she went away with her boyfriend. My parents had him once last week. I made sure to let them know, it was time for him to learn he only had one home. Shit, my son barely saw us. It's a miracle, he even knew who we were. I could hear the door close and grabbed my son and his bag. Lizzie was standing at the bottom of the steps reaching for him. He was trying to get out my arms, to go to her.

"Nana, missed you." She kissed all over his face and hugged him tight.

"My purse, please and thank you." She smacked her teeth and pointed to it. She purchased me and Rakia, a Birkin bag during her vacation. I had two already but the one she got, hadn't hit the stores yet, which made it better, when I showed it off.

Once she left, I locked the door, jumped in the truck and put the alarm on the gate. Our gate, wasn't as big as Marco's but then again, I didn't have tons of people, looking to kill me. I can see why, he updated his fence and it was the best thing he did. Especially, with her calling early this morning, saying Zaire called her again. It made me wonder how he did it, when she literally, blocked him.

****

I pulled in the parking lot of the nail salon and Rakia, was getting out the truck. She actually, had a guard bring her. I guess, she was scared and didn't wanna take any chances.

"Hello, ladies." We turned around and Rakia, sucked her teeth; where I had no idea, who I was looking at.

"Um, do I know you?" Rakia, walked over to the pedicure section.

"No, but I know her." She went towards Rak, with me on her heels.

"I see, he's not here with you."

"What do you want, Ms. Connie? Are you trying to fuck my man again for money?" I covered my mouth. This was Mia's mother. Rak, told me what she did at the hospital. I had no idea she was still in town. I took a seat at the other pedicure chair and pulled my phone out. I wanted to record how Rak, handled this. If she pushed her again, I'd probably pee on myself.

94

"Honey, he is too much man for you. Shit, my daughter couldn't even handle, what he has in between his legs." I could see Rakia, getting angry.

"What my man has in between his legs, belongs to me. I suggest you look for someone else to fuck."

"Oh, I thought after seeing him, kissing Mia and wishing for her to get better, you two were over. I mean, she is his first love." Rakia, removed her feet out the water and walked up to her.

"First off… My man didn't kiss, or wish her better. You wanna know how I know that?" She rolled her eyes.

"Because, he tried to take her life; twice, and I stopped him. But guess what?" Ms. Connie, folded her arms.

"When I get home later, I'm gonna make sure he knows, whatever decision he makes to terminate her and anyone else trying to hurt me, for him to take them out. I'm tired of everyone thinking, they can say and do, what they want to me." Ms. Connie, started walking backwards. Rak, was on her.

"And let that be the last time you mention my man's dick, or that your ho ass daughter, was his first love. She may had been in the past but I'm his soulmate. I'm the one, he craves for, when we're not together. I'm the one, he's making his wife. Me, not her or anyone else. I suggest you go say your last goodbyes to her because today, will be the last day she breathes."

"Whatttt? Please, don't tell him. Oh my God!" She went running out and Rakia, sat down in the chair. I hit send on the phone and looked at her.

"You ok?"

"I will be, when my man comes home." She laid her head back on the seat, put her earphones in her ear and turned the music on. My phone rang and it was Marco.

"Where is she?"

"Right here, getting her feet done. You wanna talk to her?"

"Nah, but I'm gonna do what she asked. Make sure she goes home after you two are done."

"Ok."

"Ang."

"Yea."

"Tell her, I'm proud of her."

"I will." He hung up and I laid back in the chair. I ain't telling her shit. He better take his ass home and do it himself.

****

"Mmmmmm. This steak is so good." I said in Rak's restaurant. We came here to eat after the nail salon, to try more of the food.

"Whoever Marco, hired for the chef, does a great job."

"I know right. But you have to try the shrimp." She had steak and shrimp, on her plate.

The two of us sat there for over an hour, eating and talking about her wedding. Rak, wasn't giving up on her relationship and still spoke about the wedding of her dreams. She wanted a huge one and after the list Marco's mom showed us, of just the family, she would have enough of them there to fill the church alone. Then you had, some of her family members, who didn't fuck with Shanta anyway, that wanted to come. Some people from her job were coming and I'm sure she'll be inviting classmates.

When Rakia came home for the summer, she was doing classes online at Harvard. Once, September came, she transferred to NJIT, where she goes to class twice a week and does the other courses online. She wasn't allowing her education to stop, regardless of what she was going through. Plus, Marco hired a nanny to help with Brielle, because he said she wasn't dropping out, either.

After we ate, I noticed someone riding by, as we were walking out to leave but never mentioned it to Rakia.

"Call me, when you get home."

"You think, he loves me?"

"Girl bye. Marco, ain't ever leaving you. Now go." I closed the door and kept my eye on the prize. I said goodbye and jumped in my car, to do what, I needed to. Its been a long time coming.

I followed the person who didn't seem to have a care in the world, at the moment. She went through town first and then, stepped out at the pharmacy. I waited and continued behind, trying not to be seen. I doubt she paid attention to her surroundings anyway, which is why, the look on her face is going to be priceless. She drove another twenty minutes and finally pulled in an apartment complex.

I was hoping it wouldn't be hard to find the door and what do you know? The place, was on the ground level and in front of me. I stepped out and checked my surroundings. With the time going back, it was already dark at five and it's no telling who's lurking in the darkness. I knocked on the door and she asked, who it was. I checked my phone to make sure u didn't butt dial Tech, and said my name. She smirked and so did I.

"Your man ain't here."

"Duh!"

"He was here earlier though and I must say, the way he took care of me, was worth the wait." I laughed because he had me on the phone, while he chastised her. She begged for her life and told them where Zaire was. They knew, he'd be gone when they got there, which is why, he called someone else, to put a tail on him.

"Yea, my husband has that effect on women. You know, what's crazy though?" I pushed past her and went in.

"I didn't invite you in."

"Oh, my bad." I walked around her place, to make sure no one was here."

"What do you want?"

"Well, I wanted you to leave my husband alone and you didn't listen. You constantly, send him nasty messages, thinking he would cheat. The videos of you playing with yourself, are disgusting. Who fucks a dildo and sends it to another woman's man?"

"He showed you."

"He's my husband and we don't keep secrets."

"Oh, so he told you about my abortion, when you were away at school?"

"WHAT?" I hated, she took me there.

"Yea, he and I, had a lot of sex, when you left him and he slipped up. I felt that big ass dick raw. He came in me and you damn right, I would've kept the baby, had he not remembered, what he did."

"I'm lost."

"What don't you get? You left him alone and he needed sex. Who you think he turned to?" My mouth fell open.

"That's right boo. The one and only, Shana. The one, you claimed he doesn't want, is the exact same chick, he trusted enough to give a child too. Regardless, of him making me terminate it; the fact he gave me one, says he had feelings for me. You can sit here and claim, he'll never leave you and all the other shit a wife says and you're right, he may not. However, he and I, had chemistry and almost shared a child. Why do you think he hasn't killed me?" I stood there listening to the shit she said and was at a loss for words. *Why didn't he kill her?*

"Oh, you're gonna cry." She must've seen how watery my eyes became.

"Do me a favor and let those tears fall, outside my door." I picked my phone up and called Tech. I had the voice of my mom, in my ear saying don't let this woman break you up, but this new revelation she told, had me ready to leave him for lying. If he loved her, he could've told me. How could he

101

keep her having an abortion, a secret? Does he love her too? I called him right up, as I stood there.

"Yea, babe."

"Did you get Shana pregnant?"

"Where are you?"

"DID YOU?" His silence spoke volumes. I hung up and her phone rang. She put it on speaker phone.

"Is my wife there?"

"Yup. Can you come get her?"

"Why would you tell her that?"

"Because its true Tech. You got me out here looking like a fucking stalker. You told me you loved me and soon as she came back home, you left me in the cold. I'm tired of looking like the bad one." He hung the phone up and I walked out, with my tail between my legs. What could I say? This time, she had me beat.

Tech

FUCKKKKKK! I yelled out to myself. When Ang called, I assumed it was to tell me the shit between Mia's, Mom and Rakia. Never in a million years, did I think she'd go to Shana's crib. I'm not cheating, nor did I, when she got pregnant but it's definitely not anything, I wanted my wife to find out. Yea, when she left me, I fucked Shana, here and there but so what. She wouldn't speak to me, answer my calls and come to find out, she had the dean move her to a different dorm. In no way, am I wrong for sleeping with someone else; however, it's something I should've told her.

The night, I slipped up in Shana, was a mistake and to this day, I still regretted it. She brings it up any chance she gets. It usually goes like, *"Why did you let Angela, keep your baby and not me. We've known each other longer."* The same shit, every time. Did I have feelings for Shana? Absolutely! I'm not ashamed to say, I was loving a stripper. She worked in my club, left with me every night and never did private parties or personal dances, in other rooms.

Unfortunately, she messed up, when she tried to get us killed, by her cousin. I understood the situation and had she told me, instead of playing me, I would've handled it. The shit backfired and I, stopped giving a fuck about her. Of course, I continued sleeping with her but she was no longer the only one and my love for her, faded.

"Shana, you can't have this baby." I sat on her couch. It was a few weeks after sleeping with her. I forgot to use a condom and thought nothing of it, like most men. Then she sends me a damn ultrasound picture, saying Congratulations daddy. I came straight to her house.

"Why not, Tech? She left you and we've been together longer." I watched as she wiped her eyes.

"That's not it Shana. I don't love you anymore."

"Why?"

"You messed up, by tryna set me up. I still fucks with you, but you ain't loyal. I can't let you have a kid by me and you get in other shit. What happens if they come after you with my kid?"

"You're telling me, that she is the only one, you want to have your kids?"

"Yes. Ang, is the only person, I want to have them. I'm not with having multiple baby mamas."

"Then you should've thought about that before.-" I snatched her up by the neck.

"Don't tell me what I should've done. You're getting rid of the kid." I threw her on the couch.

"She doesn't even want you Tech. She left you and you're still waiting for her."

"I'm sorry Shana but she's the only one, I wanna be with. I'll wait forever, for her, if I have to."

"So, fuck this kid, right?" She pointed to her stomach.

"It's not a kid. You're barely three weeks, from what the ultrasound says. Get rid of it." I slammed the door shut and left.

The next day, I went straight to her house and woke her up. I made her think we were going to eat, and took her to the doctor's office, who did early terminations. Hell yea, I stayed up all night, searching the internet for this place. I didn't sleep

105

at all and never planned to, until I knew the procedure was done.

She walked in pregnant and out, on medication to stop infection. Of course, she was mad but I didn't care. I knew, Ang would be back and I'd make her my wife. I've never cheated on her again, after the one time and don't feel the need to. What I will say is, she can cancel any thoughts of leaving me because like I always say, it ain't ever happening.

I sped over there, assuming Ang hadn't left. The door opened and out walked Shana, with her arms folded. You could see she had an attitude and I'm not beat. She tapped on my window, at the same time, I dialed Ang's number.

"What?" I shouted at Shana, the same time, my wife picked up.

"Where are you Ang?"

"Doesn't matter. Go be with your other baby mother?"

"Cut the bullshit. Where are you?"

"Tech, we need to talk." Shana said loud enough for Ang to hear.

"Did you really go to her house?" She scoffed up a laugh.

"I thought you were here."

"She can have you. Goodbye Tech." She hung up and I tried to call her back but she shut the phone off.

"WHAT SHANA?"

"Don't snap on me because she found out."

"You did the shit on purpose. What you tryna gain? Huh?"

"Obviously, she's gonna leave you, soooooo. We may as well work it out."

"You sound dumb as fuck. Get away from my shit." I backed out and drove off.

I tried Ang, a few more times and it still went to voicemail. I went home to see if she was there and surprisingly, the car sat in the driveway. I hopped out and ran inside, only to find it dark. No lights were on downstairs. I went up to the room and she wasn't there either. She could only be at one, of two places. I called her mom and she said, Ang dropped my son off and left. The next call was to Rakia. If anyone, knew where she was; she did.

"Hey, Tech."

"Where is she?"

"Tech, I don't wanna get in the middle of this."

"Rak, let me talk to her." I heard rumbling in the background.

"Stop acting like a kid, Ang. Get on the phone." Rakia yelled.

"Tech, my mom has the baby."

"I know where he is. Why aren't you letting me explain?"

"Explain what? How you almost had a kid by someone else and kept it a secret? Or how, you couldn't kill her because of your feelings? Or how about the fact, you fucked her, after knowing she's the reason, I left you in the first place? Which one do you wanna explain?" I sat on the couch running my hand over my face. I really had no reason not to tell her, or why I slept with the very same woman, who tore us apart.

"Ang, I'm sorry."

"Why didn't you just tell me?" I could hear her sniffling.

"I was scared you wouldn't come back." It was the truth.

"So, you made a decision for me."

"I'll do it again, if it kept you from being hurt, or leaving me."

"She said you still love her. Is it true?"

"Ang."

"DO YOU?" I could tell from the way she asked, it was killing her.

"Yes."

"Ok. Give me a few days to move out." She hung up and I threw my phone at the wall. The shit broke into pieces. I stood up and wiped my eyes. Hell yea, I was shedding tears for her. She's my wife and it's never gonna change.

****

A few days, went by and Ang, wouldn't take my calls, or allow me to see her. I know, she's been at Rakia's because she didn't want to run into me, at her parent's. I could've went in, but I wanted to give her time to get over it. I don't mean it in a bad way, but it was when we were apart. I would be mad too, if she told me about another nigga but I'd have to respect her choice and not get mad at the past. I drove to my mom's house and opened the door, only to hear, her and Ang, talking.

"Ang, I understand why you're upset but you have to go home."

"I want to, trust me, I do. I miss him so much but he should've told me." I could hear her sniffling.

"Ok Ang. Say he would've told you. What would you have done?" I stood there waiting to hear what she said.

"I probably would've left him."

"Then why are you so angry, he didn't tell you. Ang, everyone in this world, knows Antoine, loves the hell outta you. Didn't your mom tell you, not to let her ruin your relationship?"

"Yea, but.-"

"There are no buts, Ang. And we all know, Tech, ain't going to let you leave him anyway."

"I know." She laughed.

"The longer you stay here, the longer it's going to take for you to hear his side." I cleared my throat and pretended to have just walked in the house. My mom, kissed her cheek and left us in the kitchen. I grabbed her hand and took her out to the pool house. She didn't need to hear what we spoke about; regardless, if she knew the things going on. I closed the door and sat on the couch. She had this place, set up like a small apartment.

"Ang, I don't know why, I slept with her after you left me. I guess, it was convenient and there." She sucked her teeth.

"As far as, her having my kid, it was an accident. I had been drinking and the sex was spur of the moment. I would never hurt you like that." I walked over to her and made her look in my face.

"When I said, I still loved her, you hung up before I could finish." I wiped her eyes.

"She and I, were together for two years so of course, I loved her. You don't be with someone that long and not catch feelings. I'm in love with you Ang and nothing she says or does, will ever make me want her." She didn't say anything.

"Ang, you had me, the night at the club, when we exchanged numbers. Everything about you, was the type of woman, I wanted in my life. You're smart, beautiful, can cook and in the bedroom, you already know what it is."

"Tech."

"I'm sorry, for not telling you but this is the reason, why. I knew in my heart, you'd try to leave and I couldn't allow that to happen. You and my son, are my life, Ang. Don't you know that by now?" I kissed the new tears, falling down her face.

"This is my last time telling you, to stop allowing her access into our world. You're giving her what she wants."

"I'm not."

"Ang, she heard you on the phone and said, now that you most likely left me, she and I, should try and make it work. She wants your spot and you keep giving it to her, in a way."

"WHAT?"

"She'll never get it but stop offering."

"Why didn't you kill her?"

"Kill her for what Ang? You beat her ass and I stayed away, like you asked." After my wife beat her up at the restaurant, you damn right, I was on my way to get at her but Ang asked me not to. She said to leave it alone because she was confident in her spot.

"The day, I went over there to get info from her, you were on the phone. Baby, if you want me to kill her, I will."

"But I thought you loved her." I laughed.

"I have love for her Ang and always will. It doesn't mean I want her. Do you think if I did, she wouldn't tell you? Any chance she got to blast it out, she would, just to piss you off." She started taking her clothes off and as bad as, I wanted her, I refused to let her think sex would fix this.

"Get dressed, Ang."

"Did you sleep with her?"

"HELL NO! But this ain't happening either." She snatched her shirt off the floor.

"Fine! I'll go find someone.-" The words never left her mouth because my hand yanked the back of her hair. I wanted to choke the shit outta her but caught myself.

"Don't ever let those words leave your fucking mouth. Do you understand me?" She started crying again.

"I love you to death and if you even think about entertaining a nigga, I'll take your life and that's on my dead parents." I let go and she fell against the wall, crying. I felt bad for putting my hands on her, but I don't play those childish ass games.

"You wanna get mad and talk about fucking someone else. You got me fucked up, Ang. Get your shit and let's go."

"I'm not going anywhere with you."

"Ma, you don't have a choice." I lifted her over my shoulders and went out the back gate. I was gentle as could be, being she's pregnant. If my mom saw her crying as hard as, she was, she'd probably shoot me.

Ang, cursed and punched me in the back a few times, the entire way to the car. I could see my mother looking out the window, laughing. I made Ang, get in and dared her to get out. Once we pulled up at the house, she rushed out the car and stood there tapping her foot, while she waited for me to open the door. I took my time and smiled as she stormed up the steps and slammed the door. She was such a fucking brat, but she was mine.

I gave her a half hour before going in the room, to check on her. She wasn't in the bed, which meant she was in the bathtub, relaxing, like she did when she was stressed. I stepped in and her head was laying on the bath pillow and she had music playing on her phone. I lifted my sleeves up, grabbed the sponge and began washing her up. Not once, did she try and fight me and stood up for me to dry her off. I helped her out and watched as she got ready for bed. Instead of getting in with her, I walked out the room.

"Where are you going?" I ignored her and went in the spare room. We needed a break from each other.

"Antoine." I smirked, when she came in the bathroom and saw me in the shower. She stood there, biting her lip as she watched me clean myself. Usually, I'd snatch her up but I let her stand there, and wish she could have me.

"Tech, I'm sorry, for jumping to conclusions and not listening to you." I moved past her and grabbed some pajamas to put on.

115

"TECHHHHHH!" She yelled.

"Are you sleeping in here, because I can go in the other room?" She folded her arms and stormed out. I shook my head and laid down. I picked the remote up and started flipping through the channels. Before long, I dosed off, only to wake up the next day, with my wife, lying next to me. *What a fucking brat?*

Cara

"When are you gonna kill her?" I asked Zaire who was staying with me at some small cottage, Marco's dad, had us tucked away at. The night my brother left the hospital, my mom said it was best for me to get outta there, in case Rahmel told. I stayed with Bobbi for two days but I've been here ever since.

"Why you worried? It ain't like you can fuck the dude, you're trying to get her away from."

"Fuck you! You're the one, obsessing over my cousin because she don't want you. Then you going after a nigga, who killed your brother in front of you. Didn't you say he killed your mom too? I wouldn't even think about trying someone like that."

"But you did, when you went after Rakia. That nigga wants you dead and has a bounty out on you. So, sit your ass over there and shut the fuck up." He was getting on my nerves.

See, Bobbi told me how Marco, asked where I was and she supposedly, didn't tell him. Anyway, a few days ago, she was to go see him at the club and try to sleep with him again. Unfortunately, she never returned, which tells me, she tried and Marco, took her life for it. Word on the street, per Marco's father is, he was so in love with Rakia, that he even killed Mia, for her. Why the hell, is he in love with a retard, is beyond me. I know, she can't fuck better than me and I'm a pro, at sucking dick. I just had to make him see it and right now, the paralysis, is stopping me. The doctors said I won't walk again but my ass is determined.

I've been doing my own therapy, everyday in the bed. I try to walk but my legs feel like noodles. There's no feeling in them and if I made an attempt to stand, I'd fall. It didn't stop me from trying, though. My mom had to help me off the floor a few times. Its ok, though, because like I said, I'm gonna walk again and get my man back.

****

"Cara, you have to be quiet." My mom said, putting my wheelchair by the car door. It was dark out, and no one was on the street. We had to come see my grandfather to get some

118

things, my grandmother left. I was under the assumption she left everything to Rakia.

"Hurry up, mother." She sucked her teeth and turned my chair around to go up the steps. It was only four of them but she did it hard. I swear, it was on purpose.

"Why did you come so late?" My grandfather asked and opened the door.

"You know, Marco wants to kill her." She had the nerve to leave herself out.

"Whose fault is that?" I rolled my eyes and watched my mom lock the door.

"Here?" He handed both of us a brown manila envelope. I opened it and there was a letter and another small envelope.

To my dearest granddaughter Cara,

When you were born, I was excited and couldn't wait for you to get bigger, so I could take you to the park, go shopping and show you off to my friends. You were such a beautiful and charming little girl. Always the center of attention and everyone loved you. Over the years, you grew into a hateful and jealous bitch and I hated it. No matter how many times, I tried to get you to change, you only got worse.

I'm not sure, why you were this type of person but honey,

karma is going to come for you, so be ready. Anyway, I want

you to have this check, enclosed in the other envelope and

think of me, every time you spend the money. I love you Cara

and don't spend it all in one place. I had a huge grin on my

face and rushed to open the other envelope.

"WHAT THE FUCK IS THIS?" I ripped the envelope

more, as if the total would change. A small sticky note came

out.

This five dollars, is all you deserve. I'm giving it to you,

to buy a clue. You stole your cousins' money and now, you

expected me to give you something. Have a good life my

precious grandchild. I tossed the envelope, the letter and check

on the floor. My mom sucked her teeth after reading hers. I

was about to ask what it said but she came.

"You're not happy with, what grandma left you?" I

froze. She shut the door and stood in front of me. I was hating

like crazy. Rakia, had on thigh high, red bottoms boots, a brand

new looking Louis Vuitton bag, a cream sweater dress and her hair and nails were done. Hate filled my mind and I couldn't wait for Zaire to kill her. That was supposed to be me, living the life she has.

"Hey grandpa." She kissed him and ignored my mother.

"You ready to go?"

"Where are you taking him?"

"Well, since you're being nosy. My fiancé." She flashed her big ass ring.

"My fiancé, purchased a condo in the over 55 community for him. It's really nice and the way, I furnished it, makes it even nicer." She smiled at him and he stood up.

"Let me get my things and we can go."

"Rakia, you think because he's buying you all these things, you're better than us?"

"Cara, I've always been better than you but you put me down so much, I didn't see it. You spent your entire life hating on me, for no reason. Every opportunity I had, so did you. Hell, your mother was in your life and you still weren't happy." She moved closer to me.

"I know, its killing you to see me doing good, well actually great. My man, you know the one, you've been trying to steal, takes very good care of me, his daughter and our next one."

"You're pregnant again." She rubbed her stomach and smiled.

"I'll give that man twenty kids, if he wants them." My mother stood up and started walking towards her.

"If you even think about putting your hands on her, I'll knock your head off." I turned around and Rahmel was standing there.

"Did you really think, I'd come here alone; knowing the two of you may be here? It would give you great pleasure to lay hands on me, wouldn't it?" I gave her a fake smile. I looked over at my brother.

"Rahmel, how you turning on us?"

"I told you before; my mother and sister, are dead to me. Rakia and Angela, are more of my sisters, then you've ever been."

"Really, Rahmel?"

"Really. Now, be sure to keep this house up, the way grandma did."

"What are you talking about?"

"Oh, grandpa left you two, the house. I don't see you living in it long though." Rakia said looking around.

"And why is that?"

"Oh, because my fiancé is going to kill you." She gave me a fake smile.

"And you're gonna let him?" She stood behind me.

"ABSOLUTELY!" She grabbed the back of my chair and Rahmel opened the door.

"What are you doing?"

"Oh, I want you to see how it feels to be helpless, with no one to care." She lifted my chair and tossed me down the steps, making me fall out of it. My face hit the pavement and I think my arm was broke. I could hear my mother screaming.

"I wouldn't be too loud, aunt Shanta. Someone might hear and call Marco." She said.

"Why haven't you called him, yet?"

"He knows you're staying in that cottage, courtesy of his father. He's waiting for the right time to get at you. Or maybe, it's because I told him to wait a little longer so you can see, how good I'm living. Who knows?" She went back in the house and my mother was trying to help me up. I screamed out in pain when she touched my arm. She had no choice but to call the ambulance. Once the cops got there, I did, what I do best. *Snitch!*

"Officer, this woman, attacked me in the wheelchair." Rakia, came walking out with my grandfather.

"Is this true?" Rakia stood there looking confused.

"Are you serious, Cara?" Rahmel asked and I put on a show.

"My arm is broken and she did it. I want her arrested for assault on a disabled person. Look at my face. Its scraped up and I'm probably gonna have a black eye."

"Ma'am, I have to place you under arrest."

"WHAT?" Rakia yelled and my grandfather shook his head. He started reading her rights, as the EMT's put me in the back of the truck.

124

"See if your man can get you outta this one." My mother shouted.

"I tried to spare you and give you extra time on this earth, but you won't be here much longer." The way she said it, sent chills down my body. Did she just threaten me?

"Please take me to a different hospital."

"Ma'am this one is closer."

"Please. She's gonna have someone kill me." I cried and the guy must've felt bad. They took me to some spot that was a half hour away. My mom, came running in and said she'd be here when I got out.

"Cara, we have to leave." My mom said, once I opened my eyes.

"I know. But where?"

"One of the guys, I used to mess with said, we could stay with him. But Cara, he's older and you have to keep your mouth shut. Right now, he's our only option, if we want to stay alive. Once I get enough money, we'll leave the state."

"But what about my man."

"HE AIN'T YOUR MAN. GET OVER HIM!" She yelled.

"We're going through all this shit because you don't want to leave him alone. It's time to move on Cara." I didn't say another word. Maybe she was right about leaving Marco alone. It's obvious he isn't leaving Rakia, especially: if she's expecting again and about to marry him.

I agreed and told her, we could leave the hospital when she was ready. My arm was broken and had a cast on it. The doctor said it was no need to stay the night. So long for now, but I will be back, to get Rakia. She's the reason, I'm like this and I'm gonna make sure she suffers a worse fate.

Marco

"I know, you better be shitting me about my girl, being arrested." I said to Rahmel, who called to tell me about the shit with Cara. Tech and I, were outta town and wouldn't be home for a few days. I haven't spoken to Rak, since I left the house but she's still my fiancé.

"Mannnn, Cara told the cops, Rakia threw her down the steps and she wanted her arrested, for assaulting the disabled." I busted out laughing. The shit is comical and for her to get Rak arrested, only shows how petty and jealous, she really is.

"How much is her bail? Matter of fact, go get her."

"Alright. I'll call you with the bail amount."

"There won't be one."

"Huh?"

"By the time you get there. Rak, will be waiting for you, in the hallway."

"Umm, ok." He hung up and I called the captain.

"What do I owe the pleasure?" He said on the phone. This fat bastard knew, he was about to get paid. I hated paying cops but sometimes I had to. There's no way, Rak would sit in a jail cell. Not even for, two minutes.

"My girl was arrested on some bullshit. She better not see the inside of a cell. Do I make myself clear?"

"Very! She's coming in now."

"Make sure she's waiting in the hallway for her cousin."

"Mr. Santiago, we didn't know she was your woman. Had we known, you know, she would've never been arrested." He was scared as hell, just the way I liked it. See, he always had a money sign in his head, when I called but if he heard a certain tone in my voice, he became nervous. He knew what time it was.

"She won't see a cell."

"Good. I'll hit your bank account shortly." I told him and hung up. I sent a text to Rahmel and told him to let me know, when he drops her off at home.

"Tell me, Cara didn't get her locked up." Tech passed me the blunt, as we watched the woman who's supposed to be pregnant by Zaire, go in her house. Yea, we were in Connecticut again.

"Yup, and its probably because she saw how good Rak looks and is doing, so she started hating." I know if she saw my fiancé, Rak was dressed to impress and knowing Cara, she despised her for it.

"Probably. Yo, the bitch is certified crazy."

"I know and the last time, I spoke to her about getting at them, since we knew where they were, she asked me to wait."

"Why?"

"She wanted them to be paranoid. I think, she wanted Cara to see, she can't have me. The bitch took her through so much, it's probably to rub how good she's living, in her face." Rakia had more money in her bank account, than my mother, and I laced her account well.

See, I purchased businesses and put some in Rak's name; therefore, her account grows daily, along with the interest, it accrues. She had a brand-new Lexus truck and recently ordered the 2018 Porsche truck, coming out. The only thing she wanted next, was to marry me and I was struggling with it. I would love her as my wife but she had to decide what she wanted because I'm not dealing with no bullshit and I damn sure, ain't sparing the Zaire nigga.

"What's up with you and Ang? You still ignoring her?" I passed him the blunt back.

"Yup. Man, if anyone knows how much I love my wife, it's you." I nodded. Tech and I, both fucked a lot of women but he shut shit down, the minute he met Ang. Yea, he loved Shana but he lost respect for her, after the bullshit she pulled with, Zaire and Dennis.

"I can't believe she told Ang about the abortion." I looked at him.

"Why not? She's like Cara. Ang is living the life, she feels, is owed to her. These bitches are delusional as fuck."

"Yea, well; Ang better learn to ignore her ass before, she be on punishment like Rak. I'll be staying right at the condo with you, until she learns how to listen." We both busted out laughing.

****

130

It's been over a week, since the shit with Rak, asking me to save Zaire and a nigga was missing her. She had to learn forgiving people, is one thing but allowing them to live, knowing they wanna kill you, is where I draw the line. She can get over it but I'm not. I'm still killing him and the other fools, and I just won't tell her. If she finds out, I'll admit to it, let her be mad and keep it moving. Murder is nothing to me; especially, when the individual deserves it.

"You still having the party for Rak?" Her birthday was next week and Ang, had to throw a surprise bash for her. I asked why couldn't we go away for her twenty first, like her and Tech did? She said it's different because they were already married. Don't ask me the difference, because I didn't see one.

"Yea."

"I'm glad because Ang would've had a fit, she did all that shit and you cancelled it."

"I should, just to piss her off." He shook his head laughing.

"What we gonna do about her?" He pointed to the Mary chick, coming out her house.

131

"I think it's time we have a talk with her." She got in her car and we followed. Ten minutes later, we pulled up a few cars behind and saw her get out and go on a porch, full of niggas.

"Let's go." Both of us stepped out, along with my guards, Doc and two dudes, who always come with us. Hell yea, we were outnumbered but it don't scare us. We thorough as hell; plus, once we got closer to the porch, my man Rome, came over.

"What up, you two? What brings you out here?" He gave us a half hug and nodded to the others we were with.

"I need to rap with shorty who walked in."

"My sister." His eyes got big.

"Man, I'm not tryna kill her." He let the breath go, he was holding in.

"MARY!" He yelled and one of the guys went in to get her.

"What?" She stopped in her tracks. Which let me know, she's fully aware of who I am.

"Get your stupid ass over here." She moved slowly.

132

"Look Shorty. I'm just here to find out where your baby daddy at." She rolled her eyes. I stood in front of her and made sure she heard me.

"Roll your eyes again and I guarantee, your brother will be picking them up off the ground."

"Mary! What the fuck, yo?"

"I don't know where he is." She said with an attitude.

"For some reason, the shit don't sound convincing. Since you think it's a game, Doc bring my boy over." He walked to the car and brought out my pit bull. He was huge and hungry. I kept him at the warehouse and only brought him around, for reasons like this. She took a step back.

"Shorty, let me tell you what's about to happen." Her brother ran his hand down his face and the dudes on the porch, were standing up.

"You're gonna tell me where dude is, or my boy here, will eat your ass alive, right here on this street. He's hungry too, so fuck with me if you want." The tears started rolling down her face.

"Tell him, Mary. Why you tryna save a nigga, who don't give a fuck about you?"

"He's in Jersey somewhere, looking for a chick named, Rakia." The shit instantly pissed me of, knowing he made plans to get at my girl.

"What else?" She didn't speak.

"Does she smell good, boy?" I let the leash go and he sniffed her legs. She tensed up and started screaming. I saw him open his mouth to take a bite.

"BOY!" I yelled and he came towards me. Yea, his name is Boy. I couldn't think of a name when I got him and just went with that.

"Last time."

"I only have a phone number." She read it out and Doc, put it in his phone. I yanked her up by the shirt and drug her to the car.

"Yo, Marco."

"WHAT NIGGA?" He jumped.

"Can you let my sister go? She gave you the info."

134

"She did, right? Well, being she was hesitant in doing so, I think she needs to come with me, until we get him. I can't have her running to tell him anything."

"Please, let me go. I won't say anything."

"My, how the attitude shifts, when a bitch knows she may die." I tossed her in the back seat with my dog. I almost laughed at how scared she was. It reminded me of Ricky Bobby, in Talladega Nights, when his father threw the big ass tiger, in his car.

"She'll be fine. As long as, the information she gave is correct, you have nothing to worry about."

"ROME!" She shouted threw the window.

"GRRRRRRRR."

"I wouldn't yell if I were you. He doesn't like loud noises." I shrugged my shoulders and got in.

"Rome!"

"Yea." I could see stress written on his face.

"If you find him first, let me know."

"Come on Marco, I promise she won't tell." I looked in the backseat and she had her head down and was so far up on the door, if I opened it, she'd fall out.

"Can't chance it. Peace!" I chucked up the deuces and Tech, peeled off.

We drove straight to Jersey and made no stops. I didn't give a fuck if she was pregnant. Her ass, had a nasty attitude and needed to think about her life, before its snatched away. Women always thought they were tough, tryna protect their man but where's her nigga, now? Hiding out somewhere, like the punk he is. I turned around and looked at her.

"Pull over right here Tech." It was a McDonalds. I ordered a happy meal and tossed the shit in the back seat with her.

"You better hurry up and eat. Boy, doesn't like to share." He was looking at her, licking his lips.

"You ain't shit." Tech, was laughing hard as hell.

"Fuck her. My girl on punishment, which means, my dick ain't been wet. Then, this bitch here, thinks a nigga playing games and wanna talk shit. She better hope, I get some

136

pussy soon, or she's really gonna see my bad side." When I

needed pussy, I became very agitated and Tech, knew because

he was the same. We'd go around tearing shit up in the streets,

for no reason.

"I'll give you what you need." Tech and I, turned

around and looked at her.

"What the fuck you say?"

"If you're horny and it'll make you happy, I'll fuck you.

If you promise to get this dog away from me and take me

home." I shook my head in disbelief.

"First off... I wouldn't fuck you, with someone else's

dick, because my girl has the best shit out there and I ain't

fucking up for no bitch. Second... your ass is pregnant and you

offering up the pussy. What type of shit you on?"

"I'm not pregnant."

"SAY WHAT?" Tech said, now more aggravated then

me.

"I'm not pregnant. I told him that, to get money out of

him."

"Yo, I done heard it all." We drove to the warehouse in silence. I've seen a lot of shit in my life, but this is crazy.

"Get your dumb ass out."

"Where are we?" I snatched her up and pushed her inside.

"Doc, take her to lock up and make sure she gets one with a toilet."

We had an area in the warehouse, we put people at, until we figured out what we wanted to do with them. Some had cots, others had blankets on the ground and a few had toilets. This shit wasn't here for people to enjoy themselves and they were lucky to get this much. He grabbed her up and she tried to fight him. He knocked her out and ended up dragging her by the hair. My niggas, are not to be fucked with. They've been rocking with us so long; our ways have definitely rubbed off on them.

****

Today was my fiancé birthday and I couldn't wait for the night to be over. Ang, was getting on my nerves because she had me and Tech, running all around to make sure shit was

138

perfect. Of course, I wanted Rak, to enjoy it but damn. I ain't

built to set up no parties. I hadn't talked to her all day and I'm

sure, she was cursing me out for not saying those two words to

her, but she'll be alright. I wasn't ready to see her yet; however,

I would never leave her alone on her birthday.

"You ready?" Tech asked, walking in the condo. Ang,

was at my house with Rakia, getting ready for a so-called

dinner.

"Yea, I guess, it's time for her to get off punishment

but if she asks me to save that nigga again, I may kill her."

"Shut yo ass up." He walked out and I locked the door.

"I'm telling you. You're gonna get a call from me

saying, I need a clean-up at the estate." He couldn't stop

laughing.

We pulled up at the club and it was a lotta people there.

Rak, didn't know half the people and most of them, knew us.

We got out and valet, took the keys to park. I noticed Shana in

line and grabbed Tech, before he killed her. I had to tell him,

its time to get rid of her but not tonight. Its obvious, she's here to be smart. I told him to let her see, how good him and Ang are. She'll be mad, the shit she revealed, didn't split them up.

"She talking about anything yet?" I asked Doc, when we stepped in VIP. Mary, was still at the warehouse.

"Hell no but I let her suck my dick. Bro, she got some skills."

"Yo, you shot out. If you fuck, make sure you strap up. She offering her shit up to anyone. Ain't no telling, if she got the cooties."

"I'm good on fucking her. My girl, would kick my ass, if I cheated."

"Nigga, her sucking your dick, is cheating."

"But did I stick my dick in her though. Ah ha." This nigga was crazy. I sat down and let the waitress bring us a few shots. An hour later, I heard the DJ say, the birthday girl was here.

"Damn, that bitch is BAD. Who the fuck is she?" Some random guy said and I knocked him the fuck out. How did he even get in VIP? At the moment, I gave zero fucks, once my eyes laid on Rak.

"Go get your girl." Tech, pushed me.

Rak, had the attention of every nigga in the club and I must say, she deserved every bit of it. The strapless, black cat suit, showed every fucking curve on her body. She was still early in the pregnancy, so her belly wasn't showing yet. Her hair was down and she had make up on. I saw a few women with their face turned up, and I dared those bitches to say one thing to her. She looked up at me and smiled. I loved the shit outta her and I swear, God made her just for me. I guess, it's time to take her off punishment.

Rakia

I haven't spoken to Marco in over two weeks and I was devastated. I missed him so much and he wouldn't call or come to the house. When he wanted to see Brielle, he'd go to his mom's. I only found that out because when I picked out my birthday outfit, Ang, told me. To be honest, I didn't even wanna come out. Marco, didn't call or text me Happy Birthday and to top it off, Zaire has been calling me nonstop. No matter how many times, I block him, he calls from different numbers. Ang, told me to get the number changed but everyone had that number. My job, school, family members, I did talk to and a few others. Why should I change it because he's being a jerk?

"Ang, this outfit is too revealing." I asked her, looking in the mirror. She talked me into getting a damn cat suit. At first, I thought it was nice but now that I'm all made up and staring in the mirror, you could see all my curves. My body looked like a video vixen. I was never one who craved male attention and this outfit would definitely, call for men to act up.

"Girl please. You look gorgeous. Now let's take a few flicks and go out."

"What about Marco?"

"What about him? You said he didn't call or text fuck him. It's time for you to party. Its your twenty first birthday, bitch. We about to turn up." She snapped a few photos and we hopped in the truck.

When we pulled up to the club, the line was long. I was nervous because what if, Zaire knew about this and came? She told me to stop worrying and who would tell him? I agreed and stepped out. The cat calls from men started and you could see hate on the women's face. Ang thought it was hilarious, where I felt a little uncomfortable.

"Here's the birthday girl now and I must say, DAMNNNNNN!" I heard and blushed.

"Happy Birthday Rak." Ang said and gave me a hug. I almost cried.

"Ummm, your man is here." She pointed up to VIP and there he was, looking handsome as ever. I smiled and he returned his.

"Ang, let's dance."

"You don't have to ask me twice." We disappeared in the crowd. The two of us stayed on the dance floor, for a while. Then the song, Before I do, by Sevyn Streeter came on. A ton of women flocked to the floor and started dancing.

"Ang, I love this song."

I heard about, you and your other situation, through word of mouth, baby, it seems so complicated, is it over now, or did you just say it cause you're anxious, to be closer now, Cause I want you to be, all over me, truthfully, honestly, I need, I need, I need to believe.

I stood there dancing and swinging my body to the beat. It was something about this song, that captivated me. It made me think of how Marco and I, met because he definitely had a situation in the beginning.

I opened my eyes and the crowd had dispersed. *Where the hell did they all go?* The music was still playing but no one was on the floor. I looked at Ang, who had Tech next to her and she pointed behind me. There he stood, smirking, and leaning on the wall with one leg up. For some reason, he loved watching me dance. I gestured with my index finger for him to come closer. Each step he took, I bit my lip. My fiancé was so damn sexy and he was all mine.

"Happy Birthday ma." He lifted me up and wrapped my legs around his waist. The two of us stood there, engaging in a kiss, that was X-rated.

"Well damn. I guess, we know who he's taking home tonight." I stopped kissing him and asked him to put me down. I grabbed his hand and walked off the floor.

"I want you." I closed the bathroom door and pushed him against it.

"Not here Rak." I stopped and stared at him.

"You don't love me anymore?" I felt my eyes getting watery.

"Rak, you are the love of my life." He lifted my face.

"At the block party, you told me, if you had a man, he'd never degrade you and have you sucking his dick or

145

having sex, out in the open for hundreds to see." I smiled because he was listening.

"It may not be anyone in here, but there's a hella lot of people outside. I would never allow my fiancé to be seen by anyone, but me."

"Marco." He put his index finger to my lips.

"I promise, we can fuck in the truck, in the backyard or even on the beach, on our honeymoon but this ain't happening here." I nodded and he kissed me.

"Here." He pulled a box out his pocket and handed it to me. I looked at him and he smiled.

"You look so fucking good Rak." His hands went up and down my body.

"Baby, you didn't have to." I opened it and my mouth dropped. It was a diamond necklace with a butterfly in the middle, draped in more diamonds. I mean, it was blinging.

"Rak, you're worth every penny. Do you like it?" He took it out and placed it around my neck.

"I love it." He moved my hair and kissed my neck.

"I have one more for you."

"This is enough."

"Nothing is ever enough for you." He removed another box and this time, it held a pair of diamond butterfly, earrings.

"Oh my God! Marco." He took my earrings out and put the ones he brought me, in.

"Rak, I don't like living separate but." I pressed my lips on his.

"I'm sorry, for asking you to save him. I never thought about how it looked to you. All I was trying to do, was keep the peace. Marco, I trust you to keep me and your daughter safe. Do what you have to and I won't complain. Just don't leave me again."

"I never left."

"You know what I mean." He stared at me and licked his lips. Out of nowhere, you heard people screaming and gunshots going off.

"Ma, stay in here, until I come back to get you."

"Marco, I'm not staying in here. Please, don't leave me." He looked at me and grabbed my hand. He opened the door slowly and people were running everywhere. I saw the gun he removed from his waist and became nervous.

"FUCK!" I heard him yell out and pick his phone up. He called someone and told them to send his guards in and grab Tech. I had no idea, what he was speaking about, until we moved closer and Ang, was on the ground crying, with Tech's head in her lap.

"GET HIM OUTTA HERE!" Marco shouted and picked Ang up off the ground. Blood was everywhere and she couldn't stop crying. Two guys picked Tech up and ran out the side door with him. More gunshots went off and Marco pulled me down and had me and Ang, slide under a table.

"What happened?" I asked and before she could speak, two guys snatched us up and took us out the same door, they took Tech out of. They put us in a truck. Marco hopped in the front and sped off. We were going so fast, I had to tell him to slow down.

"What happened Ang?" He asked still weaving in and outta traffic. He was keeping up with the truck, Tech was in.

148

"She shot him. We were standing there and she pointed the gun at me. He jumped in front of me and… and… she shot him. Oh my God, he might die because he was saving me." She was hysterical.

"Who shot him Ang? Who did it?" Marco asked and the car stopped. We were already at the hospital.

"Shana. Shana shot him."

"Let's go." He helped both of us out. I placed my hand in his and he squeezed it, tight.

"Ma, get to the hospital." She must've asked him why.

"Tech, was shot." You could hear her screaming through the phone.

"Marco, he can't die. Please say he's gonna be alright. What am I gonna do without him? He can't leave us." She fell to her knees, against the wall.

"Ang, he's not gonna die. You're right, he won't leave you and my nephew. He's gonna be fine." He hugged her, then left me standing there and walked to the nurses' station. I don't know what he said, but she took him in the back.

149

I sat there next to her, letting a few of my own tears fall. How could I not be upset? He's like my brother. If he dies; Ang, is gonna be no good. I looked over at her and she seemed to be in shock. I looked down and blood was coming from in between her legs. I moved her legs and checked over her body. There didn't seem to be any wounds. I called the nurse over and she asked if Ang were pregnant. I told her yes, and a doctor came and placed her in a wheelchair. She started screaming, which Marco must've heard because he came running out. I told him what happened and he blew his breath out. They ended up sedating Ang, in order to take her upstairs. A few hours later, Tech was still in surgery and Ang had lost the baby. The doctor said, the shooting may have caused so much stress, the baby couldn't take it.

Lizzie came and she was a mess, as well. She went to the nurses' station, every twenty minutes to get the update on Tech. Marco, was leaning on the wall and so were the other guys, he had on his team. Everyone was waiting to find out, how Tech was and poor Ang, was upstairs, asleep. They did a

DNC on her, to make sure she didn't get any infection and the medication had her knocked out.

"The family of Antoine Miller." Marco grabbed my hand. Me, him and his mom walked over to the doctor.

"Mr. Miller, was shot in the stomach and once in the chest. We were able to remove both bullets and stitch him up. He's going to be in pain for a few weeks but he's gonna pull through."

"Is he awake?" Lizzie asked.

"No, he's in the recovery room. As soon as, he's in his own room, they'll take you up." He shook all of our hands and walked away. Marco told everyone to take it down for the night and come see Tech, tomorrow. Once they all left, Marco sat down in the chair and rested his head against the wall. I didn't know what to say so I sat on his lap and hugged him.

"MARCO!" Some woman yelled and all of us turned around.

"Yo."

"Really!"

"Really what?" I was as confused as him. Who is this woman and why is she questioning him?

"You have me take you to the back for Tech and then, you in here with some bitch." Whoever she was, her ass was big mad.

"Get up Rak."

"Calm down. I got this." Him and Lizzie smirked.

"Hi, I'm Rakia; Marco's fiancé." She sucked her teeth.

"I'm not sure why you're out here screaming his name, the way you are but I suggest you pipe down." She was about to say something.

"I'm not done." I stepped closer and Marco stood up.

"We all appreciate you, for taking him to the check on his brother but that's all it was. Whatever favor you assumed would happen, cancel it. My man, is no cheater and if you give out those type of favors, helping families who have a patient here, I think your boss should know." The girls' mouth dropped open.

"I'm not going to mention it because snitch doesn't run in my blood. However, if you EVER!" I shouted.

152

"Ever in your life, come for my man again, let's just say, shit won't be nice. Now have a good night."

"Bitch." I heard her say, under her breath.

"Bitch?" I turned around.

"Look, its my birthday and I really am trying to help you, make it another day on this earth. If you call me out my name one more time, I'll have no choice but to allow my man to exterminate you. Now, like I said, have a good fucking night." She looked at me, then Marco and stormed off. Marco pulled me close.

"I'ma beat that pussy up so good later, you're gonna be begging me to stop."

"I'm ready." He smiled and kissed me.

"Good job, Rak. Next time though, talk more ghetto and hit her." Lizzie said, making us all laugh. As if my night couldn't get any worse. My father was here. His clothes were dingy as hell and he looked like shit. He never looks this bad when he came out, as far as I know.

153

"Rakia, I was calling you." He said and came running over to me. I left my phone at home, so if he did call, I wouldn't have known.

"What's wrong? Why are you shaking?" I wiped the tears falling down his face and fixed his shirt. He may not be living right, but he's still my father.

"Rak, your mom passed away an hour ago." Lizzie covered her mouth and I felt Marco's arms on my waist.

"WHAT?"

"She overdosed."

"No. No. No. She couldn't have. Marco, she was getting clean and promised, to meet Brielle. There's no way she's dead. Why are you lying?" I started punching my father in the chest. I felt my body being lifted in the air.

"Calm down ma." He closed the bathroom door and locked it.

"Marco, she was supposed to get better. I wanted her to meet Brielle and you. How could she do this?"

"Rak, I'm sure she tried to kick the habit, but it's hard. I've seen a lot of people lose the battle."

"But, all these years, she's been fine and… and…"

"I know baby." I cried in his arms. My mom died, Tech got shot and Ang, lost the baby. I hope nothing else went wrong because I'm not sure my heart could take it.

Marco

"I'm taking her home. You staying, right?" I asked my mom who was hugging Rak.

"Yea. Rakia, I'll be over tomorrow." She nodded and we walked out together.

"Babe, I have to stop by Ang's parents' house." She nodded and laid her head on my shoulder. I stepped out the car and knocked. It was late, so I'm sure they were asleep.

"Marco? What are you doing here?" Her dad asked.

"Tech, was shot tonight and Ang, is at the hospital. She lost the baby." Her mother came down the stairs as I mentioned Ang. I could see her crying.

"We're on our way. Where's lil man?"

"I don't even know. He's probably with the nanny." They shook their heads and I promised to go check for them.

I made the stop at Tech's house, used my key to get in and grabbed my nephew. The nanny was there, but I also knew, if the roles were changed, he'd be picking Brielle up. Rak, got in the back and held him as he slept. Once we got home, I took him from her and laid him in the room with my daughter. Yea, we had a nanny too. Rak, was working and in school, so we had to make sure my daughter was taken care of, if I wasn't here or my mom wasn't available.

"Rak, you have to shower." She was balled up on the bed.

"I don't want to." I stood her up and unzipped the outfit, from the side. She stepped out and I had to smile. My girl had no panties on, or a strapless bra.

"So, we leave the house without panties and a bra?" We walked in the bathroom. I grabbed one of those clip things and placed it in her hair. Some still came out but the majority of it, was up.

"I thought my man, would like this." She stepped in the shower.

"Always." I made my way in with her. I grabbed the soap to wash us up and she stopped me.

"I want you to fuck me." My eyes got big. It wasn't a thing for me to do it, because we do all types of fucking.

Sometimes, I think her ass is freakier than me. I guess the way it came out, sounded crazy, coming from her.

"If that's what you want." I didn't do any foreplay and lifted her up.

"You sure?"

"Yessssssssssss." She screamed when I rammed inside of her. Her teeth were in my shoulder and her nails were digging deep in my back.

"I'm cummingggggggg Marcooooo. Shitttttt." Her juices were all over my dick. The shower was on, but I still felt it.

"Fuck me back Rak." She started popping up and down and my ass came fast as hell. I put her down, shut the shower off and took her in the room.

"I had to get that out. Now, it's time to make up for two weeks." She laid on the bed and spread eagle.

"I missed you Papi."

"I missed you too Rakia Santiago." She smiled and wrapped her arms around my neck. I loved the way my last name, sounded with hers.

"A mi me gusta cuando tu me lo metes bien duro metemelo bien duro." (I like it when you fuck me hard. Fuck me real hard.) I swear to God, every time she spoke Spanish, I got harder. I didn't want a Spanish chick at all. Its just the way she spoke it, did something to me, every time.

"You got it." I pushed my way in again and was about to tear her pussy up but she stopped me.

"Get rid of that other condo. If you get mad, sleep in the basement or another room but don't leave me again."

"Anything for you." I moved in and out slow; watching her facial expressions, show every emotion she felt, when I hit her spots. This woman is gonna be my wife soon. Fuck a wedding, we can go to the courthouse. I need her as Mrs. Santiago, ASAP.

****

"Where's Ang?" Tech asked when I walked in the room. My mom said, her and lil man are the only ones he's been asking for, besides me and Rak.

"Tech."

"Is she ok?" I didn't say anything.

159

"FUCK! I have to see her." He tried to get out the bed.

"ANTOINE MILLER, GET BACK IN THE BED!" He

looked at my mom and knew not to test her.

"Ma, is she ok?"

"Son, listen." She moved closer to him.

"Antoine, you were shot and somehow, she fell and.-"

"Nah, don't tell me that."

"Tech, she miscarried." His head fell on the bed and I

could see his eyes getting watery. He wanted this baby to be

his daughter, so I knew he would take it hard.

"Where is she?"

"They had her medicated."

"WHAT? NO! MARCO, GO CHECK ON HER,

PLEASE!"

"Relax Tech. Your machines are going off." My mom

was trying her hardest to keep him calm.

"Marco, go get her. She doesn't take medication

because she's scared of being addicted. Go get her, please." I

ran out and asked the lady at the nurses' station for her room

number. We had just walked in when he woke up, so Rak and I, didn't have the chance to see her yet. I pressed the elevator button and took it to the fifth floor. When I made it to the room, her parents were sitting at her bedside.

"Is he ok?" Ang popped up the second, I walked in.

"Yea, and he's asking for you." She took the covers off her legs and tried to stand. Her father had to catch her from falling. Her mom, had the nurse bring a wheelchair and we all took the elevator to see Tech.

"Baby, you're ok." Ang, jumped up too quick and leaned over in pain.

"Shit!" He shouted. Now he was trying to get up.

"I thought you were dead and.-" She moved slowly to him.

"Shhhhh. I'm ok, Ang. How are you?"

"I lost the baby."

"I know. They didn't give you any medicines, did they?"

"Yea, but it was to make sure, I don't get an infection. I won't let them give me any pain medicines."

"Good and I promise, to get started on making another baby, when I'm better."

"Oh, hell no! Let's go Rak." I hated when they spoke like that. Ang, waved me off and got in bed with him.

"Where's my son?"

"You already know." He laughed.

"Don't be letting Brielle hit on him. You know, she bullies my baby." Ang be over reacting. Brielle is six months old and she does run shit in the house, but she's being extra.

"Rak, why are you so quiet?" I cleared my throat and asked my mom to take her down to the cafeteria. She was supposed to go see her mother's body this morning, but refused. Her father identified her, however; he wanted my girl, to get one last look at her. I waited for them to leave.

"Her mom died last night." Tech, shook his head and Ang, started crying.

"She overdosed."

"Damn!"

"How is she? Her mom promised to get better and Rak, was banking on her meeting, Brielle. This has to be killing her."

"It is. She's been quiet all morning. I think with what happened to you two, her grandmother and now her mom, it's a lot for her to take in." We all sat there in silence for a while. Ang's parents left and said they were going to get lil man and Brielle, from the house. I appreciated it, for sure. I ended up, calling the nanny and told her, to take them over to Ang's parents' house, instead. They didn't know where I lived and its too much, trying to explain. Its not that far but they had to go through a gate and all that. Its better to have them dropped off.

"What happened?" I finally asked. Ang, had fallen asleep next to him. He never got the chance to answer because this motherfucker walked in.

"Hey." My father spoke and both of us, sucked our teeth.

"How are you?"

"Fine."

163

"What the fuck are you doing here?" I wasted no time asking him. Shit, me and my pops were never close but he knows we don't really fuck with him now, on the strength of Shanta. Her and Cara, caused too many problems and his ass, helped hide them. Well tried because I found out where they were and was waiting on Rak, to tell me she's ok with me killing them. Every time, o made the attempt to do it, its like she knew and would find a reason to make me stay home.

"I didn't come to argue. Just wanted to check on you."

"Baby, I brought you a soda. Oh, I'm sorry. I didn't know anyone else was in here." Rak handed me a drink.

"Wow! You're beautiful." She blushed and extended her hand for him to shake.

"Thank you. I'm Rakia, Marco's fiancé and you are?" By now, Ang woke up and my mom was coming in the room.

"His loser ass father. Rakia, don't shake hands with the man who's been helping your aunt and cousin stay hidden." My mom never held back when it came to him. Rak pulled her hand away and I sat her on my lap.

"Well it looks like you both did a good job on women but what I want to know is, why are you settling for one? I mean, pussy is everywhere." *What the fuck is wrong with him and why is he talking this stupid shit?*

"Excuse me!" Ang sat up and you could see how aggravated, he made her.

"I'm saying Marco. I've seen Cara and she's gorgeous. Why won't you be with her instead of this one? The one who has you in a ton of shit, over her." He pointed to Rak.

"Is that how you feel Marco? Do I have you in a lot of stuff?" I placed her on the seat next to me and stood up. She pissed me off, even entertaining his comment. I'll deal with it later though.

"Don't get mad at me because you were fucking cousins." My mother stood in front of me.

"And Tech, isn't she the one, you cheated on, too? It's obvious you two can't stay faithful, so why be with them?" Tech tried to stand up and grabbed his chest.

"Nah, I got this bro. Stay in the bed."

"You got two point five seconds to go, before I lay you the fuck out."

"MARCO!" Rakia shouted and my mom told her to be quiet, in a nice way. I guess she took it wrong because she stormed out.

"Look at her. She can't even deal with someone telling her to shut up. How are you gonna train her, to stay in a woman's place?" I chuckled and hooked off.

I tried to give him the benefit of the doubt. This is another reason, I didn't get down with him. He knew how to get under my skin. Everything he said was uncalled for and to hurt the girls, but why? He never met them, nor did they insult or disrespect him. I stepped over him and went to check on Rak. She had a lot going on right now and I didn't want her alone. I walked past an empty room and saw her standing at the window.

"If I leave you alone, will it stop all the drama going on in your life?"

"WHAT?" She turned around and had tears in her eyes.

"Your father said.-"

166

"I don't care what he said. Rak, I don't know what his reasoning is, for tryna hurt you and Ang. As far as the drama in my life, it has nothing to do with you. Two women couldn't let go, one, is a got damn stalker and Zaire, is Dennis brother. He was bound to come after me, for taking his brother away."

"Did you kill his mother?" I stared at her. Why was she asking me about this? I never told her anything, regarding the shit with his mom.

"Rak, when I handle business, you'll never know or be a part of it."

"It's the reason, he wants me dead Marco. You took people away from him and he's trying to return the favor. How could you put me in the middle of it?"

"HOLD THE FUCK UP!" Now I was pissed. She backed away.

"Once again, you're taking sides in shit you know nothing about. I never put you in the middle of anything, he did. The nigga is dangling your life as a pawn to hurt me. You think, I like not being able to find him?"

"Marco."

167

"Don't Marco me. You think, I want you on these streets, knowing he could be anywhere and waiting? You mean everything to me Rak but all you seem to worry about is him."

"I'm not worried about him. I don't care if he dies."

"THEN FUCKING ACT LIKE IT." I went to leave and turned around.

"I'm not having this fight with you over and over. Rak, if this ain't what you want, then let me know." She walked over to me.

"I'm not about to let you speak to me anyway you want to." I grabbed her arm

"I'm not disrespecting you at all. I'm keeping shit a hundred, like I always do. But you don't like to hear when you're wrong. You know what? Rak, I can't do this."

"Do what?"

"This arguing all the time. All I want to do is protect and love you but you're pushing me away and I don't know how many more times, I'm gonna come back."

"Ummmmm. Ok then."

"Ok what?"

"I'm sorry for making you feel this way. It's not my intention to hurt, criticize or make you feel like I'm choosing someone else over you. You are my everything as well but I know I'm losing you and I'd rather walk away now, then stay and make you hate me."

"Rak." She wiped her eyes and stepped out the room. I went in the room with Tech and he could tell shit wasn't right.

"I can't do this shit no more." Ang and my mom looked at me. I looked around and my father was gone.

"What shit?"

"I'm done with Rakia." They all had a sad look on their faces. I gave him a hug, kissed Ang on the cheek, said goodbye to my mom and left. Rakia, may be the only woman, I want but this back and forth shit, is not something I'm going to continue dealing with. Maybe, its best we go our separate ways before we hate one another, like she says.

Rakia

My heart was literally broken, listening to Marco say, he couldn't be with me. The arguing is too much and I agree. I love him so much that leaving him, is the best choice for now. If I didn't, Zaire was going to kill me. People probably think I'm crazy, or feel Marco can't protect me but it's far from the truth. I know in my heart Marco, will do and has done everything to keep me safe, when I wasn't hiding from him. However, he can't be with me 24/7, which is why I told Zaire, I'd leave Marco alone. He said if I did, Marco would no longer want to kill him and he wouldn't want to kill me.

At first, I refused to listen to him. My fiancé wouldn't dare let Zaire get to me. Unfortunately, he called one day I was out and described my entire outfit. The guards were there but he informed me, they wouldn't get to me fast enough, if he shot me with a sniper gun. I was nervous and scared to death because my daughter was with me. How could I allow him to kill me, with my child here? Therefore, the decision I made with Marco, is for our own good.

"She's so pretty Rahmel." I spoke of his daughter. His girl gave birth, the day my mother passed. They say, when one dies, a life is born.

"Thanks cuz. What's up with your moms' funeral?" It's been a few days and I have yet, to set up services. Her and my dad weren't married so it was up to me, since I'm her only child.

"I don't know. I've been going through so much, I haven't thought about it."

"You do know, she can't stay in the freezer forever."

"RAHMEL!" His girlfriend, Missy shouted.

"I'm going to do it today, I guess."

"You guess? Rak, what the fuck is going on with you?" I just broke down crying.

"Yo, are you busy?" I heard him ask and looked up. He was on the phone with someone.

"Nah, Rak is here and she broke down crying. She keeps saying nothing's wrong but I can't tell." He handed me the phone.

171

"What's up Rak?" Marco asked and I continued crying.

"It's so much going on and I don't know what to do. My mom is still in the morgue, you and I, aren't even speaking and I haven't eaten anything, since the day we argued. I'm at my breaking point Marco and all I want to do, is run away. This life is too much for me. Everyone I love, has left me and-." I wiped my eyes.

BEEP! BEEP! I looked and he hung up. *Typical Marco.* Rahmel stood up and hugged me tight. Missy came over and did the same.

"Rak, I'm sorry. I had no idea you two weren't speaking."

"It's ok. Can I lay down for a little while?"

"Yea, come on." Missy took my hand and guided me to the spare room. After I moved out from Rahmel's other spot, he brought a four-bedroom house with Missy. I loved the area it was in and how she decorated it.

"Rak, I know we just became friends, not too long ago but if you ever wanna talk, hang out or just vent, I'm here." I nodded and went to lay in the bed.

"I'm sorry for crying and.-"

"Don't apologize. Sometimes, life gets rough and we need to have a meltdown. I had one after giving birth."

"You did."

"Yea. I thought Rahmel wouldn't love me the same because I gained weight. Then he cut his mother and sister off. I assumed it was my fault and I had my own shit going on in my head. It was a lot." I sat my phone on the nightstand and got under the covers.

"Thank you, Missy. I really appreciate knowing, I'm not the only one who's gone through this."

"No worries. I'm gonna cook and you're gonna eat. The baby can't feed itself." She gave me another hug, shut the light off and closed the door. It took me a while to fall asleep but when I did, it felt peaceful. Unfortunately, it didn't last long. I felt my body being lifted off the bed and popped my eyes open.

"Marco? What are you doing here?" He carried me down the steps, out the house and to the truck. The guard pulled off and he ran his hand through my hair, as I laid on his lap. Once the truck stopped, he carried me in the house, locked the door and set the alarm.

"I just want to go to sleep." I headed up the steps.

"Give me a minute." Marco came behind me and walked in the bathroom. I could hear the bathtub going and him calling me.

"Come on ma." He took his clothes off and helped me do the same. I sat in front of him and my head rested on his chest. Neither of us, spoke a word but you could tell we were in deep thought.

"I miss the way we used to be. The long nights on the phone, were entertaining and fun. No one bothered us and we were happy." He massaged my shoulders, as I spoke.

"I'm sorry for everything Marco. I don't know what to do anymore, to make anyone happy." I started crying again. He nudged me forward and had me turn around. I was now on his lap but we weren't being sexual.

"You do make me happy Rak. But the constant arguing, back and forth, is too much." I nodded.

"Then why can't we be together?" He blew his breath out.

"Ma, you don't know what you want."

"Yes, I do. I choose you a million times. Please don't leave me. I don't think I can take it. Marco, I'll do anything to keep you in my life." He just stared at me.

"Marco please."

"When is your mother's funeral?" I was flabbergasted he ignored my plea to stay with me.

"I don't know. Maybe this weekend." I went to stand and he pulled me down.

"Marry me next weekend."

"Huh?"

"You heard. If you really wanna show me you're in this, then marry me next weekend."

"Ummmm." It seemed like she was hesitant and I wasn't feeling it.

"Ok then. I guess we should part ways."

"No, no, no. I wasn't saying no, it's just, my dress isn't done, the guests aren't going to be able to make it, on short notice and.-" He pressed his lips on mine.

"Minor things baby."

"That's not minor." I pointed to his dick.

"No but you can handle it."

"Sssssssssss. Fuck, I so need this right now." I moaned out, when he mounted me on top.

"Are you gonna marry me?" He guided my hips in circles, then back and forth.

"Yessssss." My head fell back and I came all over him.

"Rak, fuck your man." I stood on my feet and water splashed all over the floor.

"Yea Rak. Make me cum." I did like he asked, squeezed my vagina muscles and he grabbed my hips tight. I began kissing him and his man woke up again. This time he let the water out and turned the shower on. He loved seeing the way my hair stuck to my face and how the water sprayed down on my skin. He was truly infatuated with me and I felt the same way, towards him.

****

"This is it Rak." He dried my body off and got in bed with me.

"No more asking about him. No more, getting angry, when I call you out on shit. And no more listening to others and taking it out on me."

"I'm going to try my hardest."

"Husband or not, your ass won't get no dick for a long time."

"As long as you're my husband, I'll wait for it." He smiled and made me sit up.

"Do you need to see someone?"

"About?"

"We're not gonna ignore the breakdown you had. You had me stressed out."

"I did?"

"Ma, I've seen you upset and nervous. But this time, you had me scared. I thought you would take your life or run away and I'd never be able to find you."

"I'm overwhelmed with everything. Then Zaire told me if I leave you, he'll stop bothering me. Marco, I can't stay away from you and if he kills me for loving you, that's a chance, I'm willing to take."

"SAY WHAT?" He moved me off his chest and told me to tell him everything.

After I did, he was upset but it felt like a weight was lifted off my chest. I stood up and went to the bathroom. As I sat in there, my stomach began to rumble. My ass was so stressed out, I didn't eat because food was the last thing on my mind. I finished and came out to find him getting dressed.

"Where are you going?"

"I need to find him."

"Can you do it tomorrow?"

"I have to get him Rak."

"Tomorrow please. I've missed you." He stared at me and eventually removed his clothes.

"I hate that you can make a certain sad face, and I melt in your hands. What did you do to me?" He came over and scooped me up.

178

"I have to remember which sad face because the other ones, obviously have no effect on you." He started laughing.

"They do but this last one you did, gets me every time." He put me down in the kitchen and opened the refrigerator.

"What you want?" He pulled out a few containers.

"Where did you get all this?" I opened one box and it had lobster and other seafood in it. Another box had a bacon cheeseburger with cheese fries and the list goes on and on. He literally had ten, take out boxes on the counter.

"When you said, you hadn't eaten, I told my mom and Ang to bring you food. I guess they brought all this." I instantly started crying. He ran over to me.

"You ok? Is it the baby?" He looked at my stomach.

"No. I'm fine. It's just, around this time, almost three years ago, I felt like no one in the world loved me. I couldn't pay anyone to be nice to me. Now, I have you, Ang, Tech, your Mom and a few of my family members, who will do anything for me. I love all of you so much; especially you." I wrapped my arms on his neck.

"And I love you more than you could ever know." We engaged in a deep kiss until he pulled away, to get one of the containers out the microwave.

"Eat."

"I don't want that." It was a cheesesteak. He put another container in and took it out, when the microwave beeped.

"Eat." It was a lobster tail. He dipped it in cocktail sauce and fed it to me.

"Mmmmmm. So good." I sucked the sauce off his fingers.

"You play all day Rak." I picked up a piece of shrimp and fed it to him. He sucked on all my fingers.

"Now who's playing?"

"Ima play in the pussy, if you keep fucking with me." I opened my legs and he licked his lips. All I had on was a robe; therefore, he had easy access.

"After you eat some more, I'm gonna eat. Hurry up." He and I, sat in the kitchen heating up all the food and picking through it. This is exactly how I wanted my life to be. Quiet, stress free and with my husband and kids. What else could a woman ask for?

Tech

"Tech, you didn't have to come." Rakia said at the repast of her mother's funeral. My chest was still fucked up but she's like a sister to me. What I look like, not being there for her?"

"Rak, I'm good." I took a seat at the table.

"You sure?"

"Yea. Are you ok?" She shrugged her shoulders. I swear, her and Marco, have been together too long. He does the exact same shit.

"I'm glad its over. She was suffering with trying to get clean. Marco said, its hard to stop, once you start."

"Yea, it is. How's your dad?" We looked over at him, sitting by her grandfather. He appeared to be ok, but like her, he lost his mother and girlfriend, or should I say, wife. Married or not, they had that common law marriage, shit going on.

"He says, he's ok."

"What do you think?" She took a seat next to me. I saw Ang, talking to people and making me a plate. Marco, was on the phone but I knew who he was speaking to and what it was about.

"He wants to be here for me, so he agreed to go to rehab, after the repast. I'm gonna ask Marco, if he can pay for it?"

"Rak, look at me." She had her eyes on her dad and then turned to face me.

"Marco, don't care how you spend his money, as long as, it ain't on another nigga."

"I know but.-"

"But nothing. Not only did he set you up with your own bank account, you're the mother of his kids, and the woman he's making his wife. Stop being worried about what he'll say if you dip in the money. He doesn't care."

"Yea, you're right. Let me tell my dad, I'll drop him off. He was gonna ask my grandfather because I thought, it would be hard to ask Marco." She walked over to their table.

"Its set. When do you wanna do it?" Marco asked, when he came back in.

"Tonight." He nodded.

"How is Rak, doing?" I asked because she'll tell me anything. He turned to look at her and smiled. He had nothing but love in his eyes for her. I'm not even sure Mia, had him the way Rakia did.

"She says she's good, but I think it hit her, all at once. We were going through some shit, her grandmother and mom died, and the shit between you and Ang, took a toll on her. With so much going on, its no wonder, she had the breakdown."

"Damn."

"I know. I'm taking her to see someone, after we get married. She has a lot of hate in her heart for Cara, and confusion about the way her aunt treats her now, then growing up with her grandmother and some other shit. My girl ain't crazy by a long shot, but she definitely needs to speak to someone. Shit, you know me nigga. I'll kill everyone she's ever had a problem with and won't give a fuck." And there he goes shrugging his shoulders again.

"You always killing someone." Ang said and put a plate in front of me.

"You should've been dead. Had my brother not fallen in love with you, I would've ran you over."

"That's because he loves how, I ride his.-"

"I'm out, yo." She busted out laughing. If ever she wanted to make him leave, all she had to mention was us having sex. He never had an issue with discussing other bitches but because she's like his sister, he hates it.

"Where's my son?" I couldn't turn around as fast, to see where he was.

"My mom is feeding him."

"Ang, you know I love you right?" I put some greens in my mouth.

"Tech, what's wrong?" She turned to face me.

"Nothing babe. I have to handled something tonight."

"Tech, you're not supposed to be outta bed and you're going out. What's so important that you can't wait?"

"I can't allow her to breathe one more day, for trying to kill you, three times." She gave me a confusing look.

"Three times?"

"I don't wanna have this conversation here. Baby, wrap our plates up and we'll talk at home." She stood and grabbed some foil. I heard her telling her mom, we were leaving. She wanted my son to stay over and I wanted him home. I shook my head no. Ang, picked him up and walked over to me.

"You good?" Marco came and helped me out the chair.

"Yea, I wanna take them home and get ready for later."

"You told her?"

"No, I will at home. This isn't the place to discuss it." He walked out with us and Rak, came over with Brielle on her hip.

"I'll be there around ten." I sat down slowly in the truck and he closed the door.

"Thanks for coming Tech. I really appreciate it." Rak, kissed my cheek and Brielle did the same. She reached out for me to take her, but it was too much on my chest. Shit, I hadn't held my son yet.

"Uncle Tech, got you later Brielle." She kissed me again and Rak, walked over to Marco.

On the ride home, I kept staring at Ang. I couldn't believe Shana tried to take her away from me. Had I not jumped in front of my wife, she may not be sitting next to me. The crazy part is, I don't understand why Shana was acting the way she was. Before Ang, we were only fucking. The minute, Ang became my girl, her ass became obsessed.

"What do you want, Shana?" I asked when she approached us in the club. Marco and Rakia, had just stepped off the dancefloor.

"Why couldn't you love me, the way you love her? Huh? Why wasn't I good enough?" Ang looked at me.

"Shana, you wanna do this here?"

"Yes." I moved her in a small corner. Ang, was holding my hand. We were barely talking after the shit she pulled when Shana, told her about the abortion. However, I knew she wasn't about to let her know, it.

"Shana, you tried to set me up to get killed with your cousins."

"I apologized, Tech."

187

"We were only fucking afterwards; sporadically at that. It wasn't like we went home with each other every day. You see Ang, as my girl and you harass her any chance you get. I'm not sure why all of a sudden, you're in your feelings, but I don't want you. Ang, is my wife, my soulmate and nothing you do, can change that." I turned and kissed my wife in front of her.

"Unless I kill her." I looked behind me.

"Shana, how the fuck did you get a gun in here?"

"Trey, lets women do whatever they want, if you let him fuck." I nodded. His ass was fired and dead.

"I loved you Tech and you tossed me away for this young bitch. I tried to get rid of her twice already but the bitch has nine lives."

"Say what?"

"Tech, let's go. I'm not feeling her having a gun on you."

"Back up, Ang."

"Repeat yourself." I walked up on her.

"I paid someone to shoot up the cop car that night, she was arrested for fighting Cara. Then, the idiot who was

188

supposed to kill her on the highway, fucked up too. I guess

when, you need shit done, you have to do it yourself." I didn't

have time to get mad or even kill her because she turned the

gun on Ang and all I thought of, was my kid and Ang, dying.

"Noooooo!" I jumped in front of Ang and felt pain in

two spots. My body fell on to of hers. People started running

and screaming. I could hear Ang begging me not to die, as her

tears were falling on my face.

"Tech, you ok?" She was shaking me.

"Yea, why?"

"Because we're home and I called your name three times. Not to mention, the tears on your face."

"Come over here Ang." I opened the car door and turned my body, so she could stand in between my legs.

"I was thinking about the night, Shana shot me."

"Baby." She wrapped her arms on my neck.

"She's the one, who tried to kill you in the cop car and on the highway."

"I know baby. She said it, the night of the party." I had no clue she heard. I told her to back up, but she was still listening.

"So, you know what I have to do?"

"Tech, I know you used to have feelings for her." I pressed my lips against hers.

"I don't care if she was my ex-wife. No one will harm my wife and family. She is going to get exactly what she deserves."

"I trust you to handle what you need to, but please be careful."

"Always."

"Let me take care of my husband, right quick." Her hands were already in my pants, before I could protest.

"Got damn, Ang. Shitttttttt." She was taking care of me so good with her mouth, I came quick as hell.

"I love you woman." I yanked her up and we began kissing again. My phone rang, which caused us to stop. It was Marco telling me, he was coming earlier because he didn't want Rak, to be home late by herself.

"Let me clean you up first." We walked in the house, hand in hand. It took me a few minutes to walk up the steps, but my wife was on the side of me, the entire time. She gave me what they call a hoe bath, helped me put clothes on and changed the dressing to my wounds. All I could do was thank God for sending Ang to me. She was heaven sent for sure.

"I'll be back in a few." I told her. Marco came inside, shouting my name.

"Marco, please watch over him." He gave her a crazy look.

"I know he's your brother but he needs to take it easy."

"Sure, Ang. He won't be doing anything to stressful. You know, we don't let motherfuckers talk and take them out quick."

"Be safe babe." I kissed her and made my way to the car.

"You ready?" He asked and closed his car door.

"Yup. Let's get her outta the way and focus on Zaire. He's next."

"And you know this, man." He said in his Smokey voice.

****

On the ride over, to get rid of Shana, Marco talked to Rakia about wedding shit. It was funny as hell, listening to him agree to things, he could care less about. I've heard him say, a thousand times, the ceremony is for her and all he wants to do, is show up. Once he told her, to pick whatever type of cake she wanted, I knew he was agreeing, to agree. That nigga only likes chocolate. He hung up and looked over at me.

"Don't say shit." I put my hands up and shook my head.

"Bro, I don't give two shits about what she chooses. As long as, she ain't on her period for our honeymoon, she can have a million-dollar wedding."

"Yooooooo. You shot the fuck out." He shrugged his shoulders, as usual.

He parked at the warehouse and shut the car off. The look on his face, asked if this is something I'm sure about doing. Instead of waiting for him to say it, I told him, let's go.

Even if I thought about sparing her, shit flew out the window when she admitted to trying to kill my wife, twice. Marco, helped me get out and opened the warehouse door. Doc's crazy ass was here and so were, a few others. I stared at Trey, who was beat the fuck up. Blood was coming out his nose, mouth and down his head.

"Yo, this nigga allowed mad bitches in the club, for the right price. And guess what?" Doc said and stood behind him.

"What?" I took a seat directly across from Shana.

"He's the one who let those niggas in, a while back. You know, the Zaire dude, who was shooting. Talking about one of the guys is cousin but he had no clue, they came to shoot." I glanced over at Marco and he handed me his piece.

"WAIT!" Trey yelled as loud as he could, which wasn't too loud because he could barely breathe.

"What?"

"Zaire is in town and has been working with Shana. Whatever he has planned, she knows about it."

"Really Trey? How the fuck you snitching?"

"Bitch, you're the reason, I'm here." The two of them started arguing. I let one off in his dome and looked at Shana.

"Tech, I'm sorry. It's just you wouldn't give me attention and I was here first. How could you leave me in the cold?" She went on for a few minutes.

"You done?"

"Tech, please don't do this." Her cries and pleas, did nothing for me.

"I'll tell you where Zaire is."

"Where is he?" Marco stepped in front of her.

"I'm not sure of the exact address but if you find Cara, you'll find him. He's been hiding out with her."

"Thanks." I said and shot her in the face, until her face was no longer recognizable.

"You good." My head became dizzy.

"Yea. Take me home. I need to rest." It wasn't like I did a lot but my body is definitely weak as hell.

"I sure will. I'm not tryna hear Ang mouth." He dropped me off and I called my wife to come outside.

"You ok?" She asked and closed the door.

"Never been better. I need to rest though." We walked up the steps and to the room. Ang, removed my clothes, changed my dressing again and helped me in the bed. At least, Shana was no longer a factor. We just had to get Cara and Zaire, and shit will be back to normal. Oh yea, and the aunt. I can't forget about her.

Marco

"Damn, Rak. You throwing that ass back, real good." I smacked it and pumped harder.

"I'm making sure my man knows, what he has at home, before his bachelor party. Shittttttt." She came all over me. I yanked her up by the hair, put my hand on her enlarged clit and my mouth was by her ear.

"No woman, will ever, get me to cheat on you." I sucked on her earlobe and then her neck. She loved, when I did that.

"Good. Now fuck me harder." She stuck her tongue in my mouth and her bottom half was grinding on me.

"Stand up, bend over and spread those ass cheeks." She did what I asked.

"Remember who this pussy belongs to, at your bachelorette party." I went in circles, pulled out a little and rammed back in.

"Ahhhhh Shittttt. Yessssss baby." I loved hearing her moan, yell and watching her cream all over me, like she is now.

"I'm about to cum, ma." She hopped off and I was low key mad. I loved releasing inside her warm treasure. Sometimes she'd make me cum on her ass and it was fine, but inside felt better.

"Let me suck all that good ass cum, out." I got over it real quick.

"Mmmmmm. Yea, give it all to me." She was being extra nasty. My ass came so hard, I fell on the bed.

"Come on Marco, before Tech and Doc, come over here yelling at me because you took too long." I had to laugh. Both of them loved Rakia, and knew we had a ton of sex. They'd always say she keeps a nigga spent and they're right.

"Give me a minute, ma. Shit, you know how weak, your sex gets me."

"I feel the same but my party is tomorrow and I wanna go to sleep." She walked in the bathroom to shower. I could hear her turn it on.

"That's fucked up, Rak. How you going to sleep, on me?"

"Marco, I told you to wait until later, but noooooo. You wanted it now. So, when you're gone, my ass will be knocked out." She reached for my hand and pulled me in with her.

"You ready to be my wife?" I took the sponge from her and began washing her body. We were supposed to get married a few weeks ago, but she wanted to give Tech time to heal. He is my best man and wouldn't be able to stand long. Rak, is considerate of everyone and to this day, I had no idea why her family hated her; well at least two of them, anyway.

"I guessss. I mean, you did force me to take you back." She smirked and lifted her leg.

"I was giving you the option to come home voluntarily, before I went to the extreme and forced you." She smacked my arm.

"What? Shit, you know, my ass wasn't letting you go." Her arms went around my neck.

"I wasn't letting you go either but you had to learn, cheating will never be tolerated in our relationship."

198

"Trust me. I learned my lesson." I moved the hair outta her face. My girl was beautiful and there's nothing any woman can do, to make me hurt her again.

"The real question is, how many kids are you giving me?" I rubbed her small stomach. Brielle was seven months and she was now, three and a half. She was stressed out after finding out, and I had no idea why? Yea, its soon, but she should've never let me make love to her, right away. I did pull out, after she first had Brielle, but that shit didn't last long. I blame her for letting me.

"I'm not saying a number and you hold me to it. We'll let God decide for us. Lord knows, you'll have me pregnant and barefoot every year."

"As long as, you know." I kissed her and finished washing us both up.

We stepped out and she did exactly what she said, she would and got in the bed. I went in the closet and pulled out the Alexander McQueen outfit, she purchased me for the party. It was a pair of denim jeans, a t-shirt and some Buckle Monk strap boots, I wanted. The outfit is expensive as hell but these motherfuckers, were well over a thousand dollars, alone. She was still using her own money because none of what I put in her bank account, was touched. I appreciated the shit out of her, spending her own on me. However, I wish she hurries up and feels comfortable spending ours.

Anyway, she was dosing off, so I threw some sweats on, to piss her off. Boy, did she hop out the bed fast as hell, when she saw me.

"HELL NO! TAKE THEM OFF, RIGHT NOW MARCO!" I was laughing so hard, she mushed me in the head.

"You play too much. Let's see how funny it is, when I wear a short ass dress to my bachelorette party." I shrugged my shoulders and took the sweats off.

"Oh, you don't care?" Her arms were folded.

"Not really."

"And why is that?"

"Because you would never make it out this house. Matter of fact, let me toss all those short ass dresses out now." She ran over to me in the closet. I tossed her against the dresser, in the middle of the floor. Yes, the closet is humongous.

"Don't play with me, Rak. I'll fuck you up fast, tryna show my pussy to some steroid taking, built up, muscle man stripper." She bent over hysterical laughing but I meant that shit. Those niggas look like they on something.

I finished getting dressed and let her brush my hair in a ponytail. She loved doing it and to be honest, she's the only one, who's ever touched it. When I was young, I rocked a fade but when Mia cheated, I didn't feel like cutting it and let it grow. The barber only shapes me up, therefore, he doesn't touch it either. I loved the way her hands felt in it, too. She massaged my scalp and made sure to have it smelling good. I don't know how many times Tech, or the guys would make fun of how it smelled. Talking about, your hair smells like a woman. Tech had some nerve because Ang, damn sure kept his dreads tight and used wax or whatever he put in it, that smelled like a woman, too.

"I'll see you later." I kissed her lips and then Brielle. She woke up, so Rak, brought her in here to lay with her. I took a photo of them with my phone and saved it. I was in love with my family and found myself rushing to get home, a lot more now, just to be with them. Shit, no one is promised tomorrow, so I made sure to be extra careful, in the streets.

I put the alarm on the house, waited for the gate to close and drove to the hall, Tech and Doc, rented for the party. We could've had it at the club, but someone was having a party there and Tech, didn't wanna cancel it. I don't blame him. Regardless of how much money he has, no one wants to lose money. Plus, it would be a lot of motherfuckers here and we didn't need anyone telling their women. I may not indulge but if they wanted to, they should be comfortable.

"Yea ma." I answered for Rak.

"Just wanted to say, I love you and have a good time but not too good." Most women would be mad, about a bachelor party but not Rak.

"You'll be on my mind the entire time."

"I hope so." She blew me a kiss and told me goodbye. I placed the phone in my pocket and got out. Rahmel got out his car, at the same time.

"Congrats, cousin in law."

"Thanks, and you know, Missy is gonna expect you to ask her next." He and I, laughed. We all know, when women go to weddings, they get the itch. He told me, she better sit her ass down somewhere.

I stepped in and the music was bumping, niggas were drinking and there were a few women walking around. They were most likely the strippers and waiting for me to get there. I saw Tech sitting next to Doc, and some chick. She was smiling hard as hell. Little did she know, neither of those niggas were giving her dick. Shit. Ang, would be here quick, fast and in a hurry.

Doc's woman ain't wrapped too tight either. She found out about him letting the chick we had in the warehouse, suck his dick and kicked him out the house. His dumb ass, thought she wasn't home and told someone on the phone. She finally took him back a few days ago and told him if he cheats again, she would cut his dick off and turn herself in, to the cops.

"About time, nigga. Damn! I need to see some ass and tities shake before I go home. You know my girl, on strike." Doc is a straight ass sometimes but he still my nigga.

"You know what to do." Tech told the chick. She stood up and rounded up the other women. Twenty minutes later, and a few Hennessey shots, these women were doing the damn thing. They put a chair in the middle and a bad bitch came over to strip. She did all types of tricks, not to mention, her pussy was on full display. Had I not been with Rak, she would've been bent over, in the bathroom.

"You're sexy as hell." She whispered in my ear and continued grinding on my lap.

"Oh yea. You're sexy too."

"What's up then?"

"I'm good, shorty. If it was another time, maybe. My fiancé, has this dick on lock."

"Who Rakia?" I moved her back, to look in her face.

"How you know her?"

"Ummmm. Everyone knows who she is." The way she hesitated made me look towards the door. No one was there but my instincts kicked in and I pushed her off my lap. I could hear people laughing.

"What up?" Tech and Doc, were at my side.

"Shit don't feel right." I pulled my gun out and they followed.

"Oh word?" I saw Zaire and about twenty dudes standing outside in the lobby area. I let a shot off in the air, to get the attention of my boys. The music was loud, but my gun was louder. Like I expected, they all came rushing out the door and all hell broke loose. Bullets were flying, bitches were screaming and Zaire, disappeared.

"We got all them niggas." Tech yelled out and stood up. It's only been a few weeks, since he got shot and here he is, in another shootout.

"Nah. Zaire is missing." I stepped over the bodies on the ground. One of them was laid on their stomach. I flipped him over and never expected what happened next.

"I'm gonna kill you, like you killed my brother." I stood up and this nigga, was on the damn roof. All of us, started laughing. I looked at a few of my dudes and nodded for them to get up there.

"Who you supposed to be, Superman? Bring your stupid ass down here and let me show you how Dennis died."

BOOM! BOOM! Never in my life, have I been shot, so the amount of blood leaking from my body and the faint feeling, was unknown to me. The pain in my chest was excruciating. Yea, Tech told me how he felt, but it's nothing like being in the same position. I heard gunfire, as I fell to the ground.

"Shit. Rakia and Ang, are gonna kill me." I heard Tech and tried to laugh. He's right. Both of our women are gonna flip because I was shot.

"Help me, get him in the truck."

"Fuck nigga. You heavy as hell." Doc said as he held my legs with someone else.

"DRIVE THIS MOTHERFUCKER!" Is the last thing, I heard before blacking out.

Rakia

I woke up to use the bathroom and noticed Marco wasn't in the bed and it's well after four in the morning. I picked my phone up and realized there were twenty missed calls from Tech's phone, a few from Ang, and none from Marco. Of course, my ass went into overdrive. As I was about to dial Tech, the doorbell rang, over and over. I ran down the steps and Ang stood there with his mom. Lizzie had tears in her eyes and Ang, had a sad look on hers. I backed up, shaking my head. The only reason they could look this way and be here this late, is because something happened to Marco.

"Get dressed, Rak." Lizzie closed the door and both of them, followed me upstairs. I hurried to put some sweats on, still not knowing what happened.

"I'll take Brielle." The nanny came in and scooped her up. They must've called her because she doesn't stay here.

"When are you gonna tell me, about Marco?" I asked, still shaking as I put my sneakers on.

"In the car. Let's go."

"WAIT!" I ran to get my phone, in case the nanny had to call.

We got in the car, locked the gate and headed towards the hospital. It was silent and as bad as, I wanted to know, I didn't ask. The tears were rapidly falling down my face, and my anxiety was at an all-time high. I tried the breathing techniques Marco had me use, when I became really upset. They were working until, we pulled up at the hospital and the amount of dudes out here, told me something was very wrong. Regardless, of how people portrayed Marco, he was loved by many. I stepped out and watched the crowd, part like the red sea. Tech, noticed me and came over.

"Where's Marco?" He looked at Ang, who shook her head side to side, letting him know, they hadn't told me anything.

"Rak. Zaire, shot Marco, twice in the chest. He's in surgery." My body started shaking, tears flooded my face and my head, became very dizzy.

"Get a doctor." I heard Ang, ask without yelling.

"Sit, Rak." Tech helped me in a chair and I laid my head back on the wall.

"I told him to take the guards with him." He claimed it was his bachelor party and didn't think anyone would bother him. Yet, I could never leave the house without, at least, two following me. I guess he's gone this long, with no one shooting him, he figured it wouldn't be an issue. Unfortunately, Zaire found him.

"Someone set him up." I sat up.

"Who?" I wiped my tears.

"One of the strippers is friends with Cara. Evidently, she told her about the party and they set it up, for Zaire to get Marco." He stopped talking.

"What else, Tech?" He ran his hand down his face.

"They were under the assumption you would come for some reason and made plans to get you, too." I covered my mouth. Cara, was going through great lengths to kill me and the same went for Zaire, wanting Marco.

"Who needed the doctor?" A nurse said and we all turned around. Tech, pointed to me and the doctor stood in

209

front of me, taking vitals and asking questions. He said, my pressure was a little high and they would keep an eye on me, while I'm here. Sadly, they admitted me in the ER and hooked me up to monitors.

Here we are, hours later and I was still hooked up to machines and the doctor hadn't come out. When he finally came, I fell asleep. Ang, woke me up and Tech, closed the door to the room. Lizzie was standing next to me, holding my hand. I sat up and listened to the doctor tell us, Marco was shot twice in the chest and one of the bullets, just missed his heart. There was an extensive loss of blood and he needed a transfusion. He's gonna be in ICU for at least two weeks, but he should make a full recovery. I tossed the covers and tried to snatch the monitors off.

"Ma'am, we still need to monitor you."

"Fuck this. I need to see my fiancé. Take me to him." I grabbed the gun, out the back of Tech's waist and pointed it at him.

"RAK! What the fuck?"

"Take me to him, NOW!" The doctor was scared to death. Lizzie and Ang, both had a smirk on their face, while Tech, was still fussing.

"Ok. Calm down miss. I'll take you." He looked at Tech, who removed the gun from my hand and apologized to him. He disconnected me from the machines and had me follow. All of us, stepped on the elevator.

"He's being moved to ICU, now. Give me a few minutes to make sure he's set up and you can come in." I watched the doors close behind him and started pacing the floor.

"Do you think he'll wake up? What if he slips into a coma? Can he come home, if we get a nurse? Tech, do you?-" He came over and hugged me tight.

"He's gonna be fine, Rak. Remember you have another life inside you." He wiped my tears and lifted my face.

"What did Marco, tell you to do, when you're this upset?" I nodded and took deep breaths.

"Good job, Rak. Stay calm. You know, he wouldn't want you upsetting yourself like this." Ang said and made me

211

take a seat next to her. The doors opened and the doctor came out. He said usually only two people can go in, but there was only one other patient on the floor, and as long as, we were quiet, we could stay.

All of us followed and I noticed Tech, pull him to the side and hand him money. I'm guessing, so he won't tell, I pulled a gun out. Of course, I wouldn't shoot. Shit, my hands were super shaky, holding it. Marco, had taken me out in the back a few times, to practice and I did good, but then again, it was a lot calmer.

"Remember to keep it down." He closed the door. I cried staring at the way, Marco looked. There were machines in his nose, on his heart, a cuff on his arm, an IV drip and some things on his legs. His mom told me, it's to keep blood circulating, since he wasn't moving.

"Marco baby. I know you can hear me. I'm gonna be here every day, so when you open your eyes, I'll be the first person you see. God, I'm so happy, you're going to be ok." I kissed his lips and he stirred a little.

"He's gonna wake up soon, Rak." Tech said and put a seat behind me, to sit in. I wanted to lay with him, but was too scared, he'll be in pain. All of them sat on the opposite side. Lizzie had her head on Tech's shoulder and Ang, was holding his hand.

"Hi, I'm Jaime and I'll be his nurse for the day." I glanced at my phone and it was after eight in the morning. I laid my head on the bed and let her do, whatever she needed to.

"I didn't realize it was morning yet." Tech said.

"Its ok. From the looks of things, it's been a rough night." I lifted my head to look at Marco and Tech, gave her a weird look.

"Who are you again?" She pointed to her badge.

"I asked you a question and it didn't require you, to point to a nametag." She sucked her teeth and attempted to put some needle in Marco's IV. He smacked the shit outta her hand and pushed her against the wall.

"Tech, what are you doing?" I shouted.

"Who the fuck sent you here?" She was petrified.

"She's a nurse." I tried to stand in front of him, but he wouldn't allow it.

"Rak, she's not a nurse." He smirked at her.

"She isn't?"

"Nah. What type of nurse pulls a syringe out her pocket? How did she know Marco had a rough night?" Tech put the gun to her head.

"I'm gonna ask you again. Who the fuck sent you?" The girl shook like a leaf and tears fell down her face.

"I am a nurse. Some guy pulled me to the side on the elevator and asked if I wanted to make extra money."

"What guy?"

"I don't know. His name started with a Z." I covered my mouth and listened to her speak. Tech, still had her against the wall.

"What did he ask you to do?"

"To place this in some guy named, Marco Santiago's, IV."

"WHAT ELSE?"

"I swear, that's it. Please don't kill me. I only did it because my son has type 2 diabetes and I needed the money. All of my money, goes to his medication."

"How much did he pay you?" She took the cash out her pocket.

"Ten thousand dollars. Please, don't kill me." Tech, let her go and she fell to the floor, crying.

"We have to get him outta here."

"How?" I was now worried and scared to death, another attempt would be made on his life.

"Give me a few minutes to make some phone calls. Meanwhile, watch this bitch and don't let her leave. I don't give a fuck if the hospital pages her. She is not to leave." Lizzie walked over to her.

"What's in the syringe?"

"I don't know. He handed it to me, with the money. Oh my God, please don't kill me. I'm all my son has." She was hysterical crying and usually, it would make me feel bad. However, she made an attempt on my fiancé's life, not caring or worrying about the consequences.

"We will know soon enough." Lizzie picked up the syringe and placed it in her purse. The evil look on her face told me, shit was about to get real.

Tech, came in the room with the doctor, a different nurse and two officers. The doctor unhooked Marco and Tech, helped him put my fiancé on another stretcher. The IV was still hooked up and the blood pressure cuff, had to come off. One officer picked the woman up off the floor and placed cuffs on her wrists. It was sad watching them take her out, but she's not my friend and I can't feel sorry for someone who was willing to do the unthinkable for money; regardless, of how it would help her child. I would do anything too, but take the life of someone who did absolutely nothing to me, isn't something, I see myself doing.

We got downstairs and there was an ambulance outside the emergency room waiting. I looked at Tech, and he nodded for me to get in with him. Before they closed the door, Tech told them to follow him. We pulled up at Lizzie's place and watched them take Marco out. She had them take him in a back room. There was a bunch of medical equipment inside and it was top of the line too. All the times, I've been here, not once did I notice this room. Ang, looked at me and I shrugged my shoulders.

"Everything is set up and he should be fine." The nurse, who drove with us said. I was ok with her taking care of him, until she tried to kiss him.

"Are you fucking crazy?" I pushed her into the wall.

"Oh shit!" I heard Lizzie yell out.

"Not at all. I'm sure you're fucking him, just like me. I don't understand why you're mad." *Did she just say, she's fucking my man?*

"Oh really." Lizzie and Ang, stood there waiting for an answer.

"I mean, it's been a while but a bitch still remembers how good he is." I smacked the hell out of her.

"No, you didn't." She charged me and Tech, caught her.

"Genie, what the fuck you doing?"

"This bitch smacked me. I'm about to whoop her ass." Low key, I was scared as hell and hoped he stopped her.

"First off… This is Marco's fiancé and his daughters mother. Second… you were probably in here being disrespectful as fuck because you're a messy bitch. Which is the exact reason he hasn't fucked with you in years." She rolled her eyes.

"I smacked her because she tried to kiss Marco and claimed to remember how good he is in bed." Tech shook his head.

"You messy as fuck and I'll make sure Marco knows, how you disrespected her. Everyone knows, he don't play when it comes to his family."

"I apologize. Don't tell him." Now she was scared. My man, instilled fear in many and it actually was a turn on. I couldn't wait for him to wake up. I'm gonna make him angry and let him take it out on my pussy.

Tech, pushed her out and I could hear him cursing at her. Ang and Lizzie, gave me a hug and kiss, before closing the door and leaving me, with Marco. The bed was huge, so I took off my sweats and got in with him. I was very careful and placed my arm on his stomach. Even though he couldn't hug me back, it felt good to lie under him, knowing he'd wake up. I hope it was soon, because I missed him already.

Zaire

"You should've seen that nigga, hit the ground." I told Cara as we sat in this house, her mom had us in. Evidently, she was done with Marco's father and moved on. It was quick in my opinion, which only makes me believe, she was fucking, both dudes.

"Did you kill Rakia?" I turned to look at her.

"I don't know why you assumed she would be at a bachelor party."

"Because she a got damn stalker. She has to be anywhere, he is." I had to stare at the idiot in front of me. Is she serious about Rakia being a stalker, while she's the one, who's doing the stalking? If I have to hear one more story about how Rakia stole her man, I'll probably shoot myself. The way I see it is, Marco never wanted Cara and she pursued him. He hurt her feelings and gave Rakia everything and she hating like crazy. I know, women want a baller and get upset about the man they want, wanting someone else but she takes this shit to a whole other level.

"Sorry to inform you, but she was nowhere in sight."

If you're wondering how I found out about the bachelor party, it's easy. Some stripper chick Cara knew, posted on Facebook, how she was about to make a lot of money, doing a bachelor party, for a BOSS nigga. Cara hit her up in her inbox, and she started talking about Marco was the guy and she knew he would pay well. Long story short, Cara never mentioned me attending and told her, if his chick Rakia, showed up, to call her. She was under the assumption, I'd kill her and had I not gotten him, I may have.

Believe it or not, I did have feelings for Rakia. She was smart, beautiful and her heart was pure, which is why I used her, to get her man to stop looking for me. I even said, I wouldn't kill her. Naive as she may be, he must not have trusted my word and continued coming for me.

I tried to call Mary and her brother cursed me out. He told me, all about Marco taking Mary and sicking his dog on her. That's her fault though. I told her many of times how ruthless he was and once she got smart, it was on. Her brother tried to get me to turn myself in. What I look like, dying for her? She may be pregnant with my kid but how am I gonna see him grow up, if I'm dead?

"SHIT! What about the hospital? I know she showed up."

"I'll know soon."

"How is that?" I told her about the chick who is supposed to put cyanide in his IV, to kill him. I paid her 10k to do it. I only had a million dollars left in my bank account from what my brother gave me. My mother's account was frozen for some reason and I'm sure Marco, had everything to do with it. He wasn't able to do mine because it's in my father's name. I had his name on the account so when I finished school, Sallie Mae or the Navient people, couldn't take any of it. Call me cheap all you want but a million dollars is enough to last me a lifetime. I'm not greedy or lived out my means.

I finished telling Cara about the plot in the hospital. Of course, she had a fit because she doesn't want him dead. In her twisted mind, she believes Marco will mourn Rakia and come to her. I think the bitch hears voices or something. Why else would she think some crazy shit?

"Get me right real quick, Cara." She sucked her teeth as I pulled my dick out.

"Zaire, if the plot at the hospital doesn't work, leave him alone and go after Rakia." I nodded my head as she stroked me to life. I'm tryna kill that nigga but I'll tell her yes, to get her to suck me off. She wasn't that good but right now she'll have to do. After she finished, I helped her in the bed and grabbed the KY jelly. I've been fucking her since Marco, paralyzed her. The pussy doesn't get wet and she can't even feel me, but hey, it's tight and I could cum inside, without getting a disease, or worrying about a pregnancy. He really fucked Cara up and she's still tryna save him.

"Damn, it's tight." I spread her legs and went as deep as, I could. It's not like I'm raping her because she asked for it. It took me a minute to be ok with it, though. I came pretty hard and laid on the side.

I stood up and went to take a shower. I put some soap and warm water on a rag and wiped her down. The nurse would be here tomorrow to wash her. After I got out, she was on the bed scrolling on the phone, like always. I made my way to the kitchen to grab something to eat and Shanta was standing there, in just a towel. Cara is a bad bitch but her mom had it going on too.

"What?" She asked and bent over to grab some lettuce out the fridge. I literally, could see her ass and pussy. Was she doing this on purpose? I don't know why, I turned around to see if anyone was looking. Cara couldn't move and no one else stayed here. The guy who let her live here, came by, once in a while.

"Don't you think, you should put clothes on?"

"For what?" She started coming towards me. This bitch let the towel fall and I must say, she had a nice body for an older woman.

"You wanna feel inside this pussy?" I swallowed hard.

"You know, I'm with Cara."

"Ok and what can she do for you?" She dropped to her knees and blessed me so good, my knees were weak. I fell on the couch and she hopped on top of me. We started kissing and

224

before I knew it, she had my shorts off and slid down on my dick. Her pussy felt so damn good. Then she was doing some things with it. Each time she knew, I was about to cum, she'd stop and tell me to relax. Needless to say, she and I, had sex a few times before I went to bed.

"Is her pussy better than mine?" Cara asked, when I laid next to her.

"What the hell you talking about?"

"My mother. You were fucking her. So, is she?" I rolled over.

"Well?"

"Goodnight Cara."

"It's ok. She'll tell me in the morning."

"WHAT?" I flipped over.

"You're not the first man, we've shared." I couldn't believe the shit coming out her mouth.

"I had Marco and his father. Shit, my mom's been tryna to get Marco, just to make it even, but we all know, he ain't having it and neither am I. Marco, is the one man, I'm not ok sharing." I shook my head and pulled the covers up. Her and her mama, are both ho's. No wonder they mad at Rakia. Both of them, wanted to share Marco and he wasn't letting them. What type of shit are these bitches on?

****

I woke up the next day and Cara was still asleep. I hurried to get dressed, in order to meet the chick, and make sure she put the cyanide in Marco's IV. It's a shame, I can't witness him taking his last breath, but I promise to visit his grave. It will be my pleasure to not only spit on it, but to know my brother's murderer, was dead too.

I left the house and drove to the spot, me and the girl were supposed to meet at today. I paid her in advance, so she'd know, how serious it was to take this niggas life. When I pulled up, something seemed funny. I don't know what it was but my ass never left the car. I did notice a few dudes leaving the restaurant laughing. It could be a coincidence so I didn't really pay it no mind. I picked the phone up and dialed the chicks phone number. Unfortunately, she didn't answer but the message on her machine, was heard loud and clear.

"The person you reached is currently in jail for tryna kill my brother. Feel free to visit her, being she'll be there for a very long time. If this is you Zaire, we're coming for you and I hope you're ready. Oh, my brother is alive and well. You could never kill him because you're weak just like Dennis. Enjoy these last few days on this earth, fuck nigga."

I hung the phone up and checked my surroundings. First off... who the hell leaves a message like that on someone's voicemail? And is she really in jail? Did she get caught? Oh well, at least his ass won't be mobile for a while. I need to hurry up and find him, so I can finish the job. They can kill me all they want afterwards. As long as, he's dead, I'll die happy.

Cara

"Ma, you really had sex with him all night?" My mom and I, were discussing Zaire and how we both slept with him.

Yes, we shared men, if you must know. It didn't start until, I was twenty. My mom would have tricks, as I call them who would come over when she wasn't there. She tried to tell me that day in the hospital, she wasn't a ho, but I knew better. They'd see me, ask to fuck and at first, I'd tell my mom. She was pissed in the beginning but then said, we had to use what we had, to get what we want.

After we discussed how to handle the situation, she'd call a man up and ask him to meet her at the house. I'd be there half-dressed and open the door. The guy, would get turned on and try to sleep with me. I had to play the innocent role and told them, they had to pay me, in order to stay quiet. This went on, the entire time Rakia was away at college. It didn't bother me because the money was lovely. I did tell Ang, Tech paid me to stay quiet and my wardrobe was courtesy of him, which was a lie. You should've seen her face, though. *Priceless!*

My mom introduced me to Marco's dad one day. She told me he would pay top dollar for a woman like me. I was beautiful and evidently, he had a hard on for Marco. My mom told him, I was his girl, which made him come on to me, even stronger. I went over there looking for my mother and he told me to wait inside. I felt him behind me and long story short, he fucked me all over the living room. We even had a few sex sessions in his pool. Nonetheless, he paid me five thousand, each time.

Anyway, once my cousin came back home for good and showed up at Marco's birthday party, my rage grew. Bobbi, told me how Rakia, sent Marco a text message, while she was still in school, about being pregnant and not knowing what to do. She blocked her so he wouldn't know and erased all the messages. How could he give her a child and not even have sex with me? I know people think, I'm obsessed with him and I am. He was the only man who could upgrade me and make sure I was treated like a BOSS's woman.

Rakia, was slow, so why would he give her the status and not me? It was clear, she claimed, she terminated the child because she wasn't pregnant in the first place. Now the bitch, really got pregnant, has a daughter and pregnant again. Not for long though, if me and my mom, can help it. My grandmother is dead; therefore, no one is here to help her.

"Most of the night, he had a hard time, trying not to cum fast." We both laughed as he came in my grandparents' house, or should I say, ours? My grandfather left it to us and we had a few boards on the window, to make people believe it was abandoned. The shades were black and so were the curtains. We kept the lights off at night and only used the television to see. We didn't really need anything and as long as, my mom kept using what she had in between her legs, we'd have income; along with my social security check.

"He's a minuteman, right?" She laughed.

"Why are you letting him lay on you, when you can't feel it?"

"Who knows? I guess, seeing him get hard makes me feel a little better about being paralyzed."

"Cara, you'll walk again."

"How? The doctor said it's a ten percent chance, I'll leave this chair. Marco, is the only one who has the type of money to get the best doctors, and therapist to change that. Yet, he's with the stupid niece of yours and Zaire may have killed him." He fell on the couch in front of us.

"He's alive." My heart began racing, hearing he was alive.

"Really!" He started telling us about the girl, the message Tech had on the answering machine and how he called the hospital and they won't give out any information.

"The only thing you can do, is call Rakia and ask her to meet you."

"Are you crazy? She'll tell and they'll most likely follow her. Why don't you do it?" I thought about what he said and Rakia, is a forgiving person. Maybe, I could talk to her about having a meeting and becoming cordial to one another. It's the least she can do, since her man, almost killed me. My mother asked me if I was sure and passed me the phone. I dialed her number and shockingly it rung. I thought she would've changed it. Zaire told me to place it on speakerphone.

231

"Hello." She sounded cheery for someone whose man, has been shot.

"Rakia, its Cara."

"I know who it is. What can I do for you?" I stared at the phone weird, as my mom moved her hands and told me to hurry up.

"Ummm, I'm calling to see if you'll meet up with me, to make amends. I'm sorry, for leaving you in the bathroom and I'm sure, you're sorry for pushing me out my wheelchair." She busted out laughing on the phone.

"No, I'm not sorry and why in the hell, would I meet up with you?" I had to think of something quick.

"Grandma, wanted us to make up and I think we should grant her wish." She got quiet. Her and my grandmother, became really tight once she graduated high school. I know she would try and accommodate her wish.

"Fine! When and where?"

"Tomorrow at the restaurant you own." I had to stop myself from getting mad. Yea, I found out about the restaurant, he named after her and the few other places he purchased, for her too. She told my grandmother a lot and I overheard her telling my grandfather, one night, I stopped by. She also said he put millions in a bank account for her and she tried to give it back. This slow, stupid, bitch of a cousin, was living it up.

"Ok, and make sure you bring money because ain't nothing free." I sucked my teeth and hung up. How she gonna make me pay and she own the place?

****

"Thank you, Mrs. Santiago. I'll make sure it gets done first thing in the morning." I was sitting in the restaurant waiting for my cousin and turned around, when I heard someone say Mrs. Santiago. They had to be speaking to his mom because my cousin wasn't married to him. Low and behold, it was Rakia. She signed a piece of paper and handed it back to the girl. I couldn't close my mouth, after looking at her. She had on red bottoms, a bad ass Birkin bag, the clothes were most likely expensive, as always, her hair and nails were done and the Bentley key ring, she placed on the table, pissed me off too.

"Hello Cara. Did you order yet?"

233

"Yes. Sorry, I didn't wait but I'm hungry." I gave her a fake smile. She picked the menu up and waved for the waitress to come over. The bitch damn near flew, to take Rakia's order. Maybe meeting here, isn't the best thing. All she's doing is shoving her wealth in my face and I'm not beat.

"What did you want to talk about?" The waitress took the menu and walked away. I lifted the drink, took a sip and told her some bullshit.

"Cara, I'm having a bachelorette party in a week and if you're serious about making amends, I'd love for you to come." I almost choked on my drink. I knew about him proposing but they were moving too fast.

"Bachelorette party?"

"Yes, and I'm so excited. I was supposed to have it a few days ago, unfortunately, Marco isn't feeling well and I didn't want to leave him home with Brielle." I noticed how she left him being shot, out.

"You're really marrying him?"

"Yup and if you're about to tell me some stories about him sleeping with other women, don't. I trust my man and anything you say, will only be to hurt me, in hopes, I'll leave."

"I'm over it, Rak. The best woman won, so if you're happy, I'm happy." I saw the shocked expression on her face and it was hard, trying to keep a straight face. The best woman hasn't won, yet.

"Thanks. So, how are you doing? Have you been seeing a therapist?" She moved away for the waitress to put her food down. The shit was steaming hot and it looked good and expensive. There was a lobster, shrimp and a small piece of steak on it. The side of mashed potatoes were tasty looking too. I ordered a burger and fries because it was the cheapest thing on the menu. Since, I had to pay, its all I could afford.

"I'm fine and the therapist said, I should be walking soon."

"That's great Cara." She started beating me in the head about, how excited she is to marry Marco. My food finally came and one would think, she'd shut up but no, she continued.

Everything was Marco, Marco, Marco. For the first time in my life, I could go without hearing his name again.

Once I finished my food, she definitely made me pay, while no one brought her a bill. She grabbed her Birkin bag, stood up and came closer to me. She kissed me on the cheek and took a selfie with us. Was the bitch being funny and, I noticed she had the newest IPhone. I swear, I hated everything about her.

"I'm happy we spoke Cara. Its going to be so much fun at my bachelorette party. Make plans to get super drunk." She winked and walked out the store. I noticed two guys leave behind her. He really made sure to keep her protected. Hopefully, my mother will get her at the bachelorette party. Oh yea, she's coming too. You won't have me sitting there alone and being the center of attention. At least, my mom will hook off on a bitch or two, if need be.

"How'd it go?" My mom asked when she pulled up. I had one of the waitresses push me outside.

"Great! We're going to a bachelorette party." She looked at me and started grinning. Its about to be a party, alright. The only one celebrating will be us, by the time, we finish.

Marco

"When Rak, pulled the gun out on the doctor, I knew then, she'd been around us too long." Tech, sat next to the bed, telling me my girls' behavior, when she came to the hospital. I tried not to laugh but it was hard, especially; when he told me, she smacked the shit outta Genie for trying to kiss me and saying she remembered how I fucked her.

"Where is she?" I asked because it's been three days, from what he says, since the shooting and I wake up to see him and not her.

"She went down to the restaurant. Ang and I, came over to keep an eye on you and Brielle."

"Why is she there?" Rak, never had to step foot in that place if she didn't want to. I made sure it was being run correctly.

"Man, I don't know. Maybe her pregnant ass hungry. I know Ang, asked her to bring some food home." I smirked, listening to him say, she's pregnant. No, I didn't forget but I'm glad she didn't lose my kid with everything going on. Her

238

anxiety and blood pressure, skyrockets when she's upset. And seeing me in ICU, had to have, made it go up.

"Where's that nigga?"

"So, evidently, Cara knows the stripper who danced on you. She hit her up on social media and asked whose bachelor party she was doing. Long story short, Cara and Zaire, basically went off what the chick said. Supposedly, they were coming to kill you and Rak."

"WHAT?" I sat up and clutched my chest. The doctor came not too long ago and told me the stitches are still in and I'm not fully healed. Sudden movements can bust them wide open.

"Cara, wants her dead and you know, what he wants."

"Where's the chick?" He gave me a look.

"Did she say anything else, before she took her last breath?" I know Tech didn't leave her alive after this.

"Just that, she was sorry and had she known it was a setup, she never would've told anyone."

"I'm telling you the government needs to ban social media. Motherfuckers stay in trouble off the shit."

"They'll learn one day. What's up with the wedding though? You wanna cancel it or what?"

"Let me see what Rak wants. She's been waiting to become Mrs. Santiago and I've been ready to make her my wife. Shit, we can get married in this room for all I care. You know my motto."

"I know, I know, as long as she ain't on her period. Let me call her, so she knows you're awake."

"You don't have to." She said and stood in the doorway with tears in her eyes.

"I'll let you two have a moment. Rak, is my food in there?" She nodded and never took her eyes off me. Tech shut the door.

"Come here ma." She ran over and I had to put my arm out to let her know, not to jump on the bed.

"I missed you so much. Oh my God, I was scared he took you from me. Are you ok? Do you need anything?" I grabbed her face and slid my tongue in.

"I missed you Rak." She kissed me again.

"Mmmmmm. I missed this." She put her hand in my shorts and of course he woke up for her.

"He missed you too." She wasted no time locking the door and removing her clothes. The doctor told me no strenuous activities but fuck that. She sat on top of me, gently.

"Shitttttt ma. Got damn this pussy good." I let my hands go up and down her back as she rode the shit outta my dick.

"Yes. Yes. Yessssss Marco." She let go and I swore it was a waterfall.

"Make me cum Rak." It didn't take her but two minutes to do her thing and make me fill her walls up. She laid on me softly and kissed my lips.

"Can you walk?"

"Yea. Tech, helped me in the bathroom, a little while ago."

"Good. I've been washing you in the bed but it's time you took a shower." I sat up slowly, moved the covers off my legs and stood. We went in the bathroom and she took, the rest of her clothes off, started the shower and removed mine. I stepped in and she took the shower head off to wash me, so the bandages on my chest didn't get wet. I held it for her so she could put soap on the rag.

As she washed me, I couldn't help but stare and think about how good of a woman she really is. Rak, will stop everything she's doing to make sure me and my daughter are good. If she's cool with you, she'll give you her last. Again; I'll never understand the hatred Cara and Shanta, have for her.

"Don't start nothing." I told her as she washed my dick and balls. It took one touch from her, or certain things she'd do and I'll be ready to bust her walls down.

"I'm ok for now." She rinsed the soap off.

"So, that quickie is all you need?" I took the rag from her.

"Of course not. But I know you're hurt and Ahhhhhh." She grabbed the rail, when I forced my way in from behind.

"It's enough Rak? I yanked her hair and pulled her up.

"No baby. Shittttt." She started throwing her ass back. I wanted to get freaky as hell with her but my chest began to

242

hurt. Rak knew too because she hopped off and took me in her mouth.

"I swear, you're my soulmate ma." She sucked me off real good. I leaned against the shower wall, tryna catch my breath.

"You're my soulmate." She kissed up my stomach.

"My first crush." She continued kissing up my chest.

"My first everything and.-" She was on my neck.

"And my one and only true love. My body only craves you baby." We started kissing and had Ang not banged on the door, we would've had more sex in here, hurt chest and all.

****

"So, your ass done got shot up, over your soon to be fiancé." I heard sitting in Rak's restaurant. Tech and I, were with the girls and my mom. I felt Rak place her hand on my thigh. It's only been a week, since the shooting but I'll for sure, rock his ass to sleep.

"What the fuck you want?"

"Nothing really. Just stopping through." He smirked and pulled a chair up. Rak, stood up and pushed me over to the inside of the booth. Tech and I, dared Ang, to do the same. We knew my girl was making sure, I didn't fight but little did she know, Tech, is as good as, new and had no problem handling shit.

"Mr. Santiago. Why don't you like my fiancé?" We were all shocked Rakia spoke to him. After the way, he treated her and Ang, at the hospital. I expected her to sit there and let one of us handle it.

"I love my son, but I don't like him."

"Exactly! But why? I mean, he's sitting here relaxing with his family and you come over, trying to get him riled up. Never mind, he had to knock you out in the hospital, for disrespecting me and Ang." She smirked and took a bite of the burger, she had to have. My girl, was infatuated with cheeseburgers and seafood.

"Actually, my son and his mother here, took me for everything I had. You see, the empire your man has, belonged to me and somehow, he weaseled his way in and took it. He needs to hand it over and I'll let bygones, be bygones" He smiled and licked his lips at Rakia. I had to laugh and so did my mom and Tech. He was in denial on how, I actually retained my empire and getting off, on my girl.

Growing up, my father ran his little drug ring, and of course, he gave me some dope to make my own money. However, with the money, I made, I would flip it and buy more drugs on the side. I began to make more money and made a name for myself. People would seek me out, instead of my father. Yes, I still sold some of his drugs, but now, I had my own and started building. Tech, was going through something at the time, so it took a little longer than expected, to get where I wanted, without his help. Once he came on board, we took over. It eventually put my pops outta business but shit, I can't help if people wanted to fuck with me and not him. It took me a year and a half to get *"The Plug"* status but it was well worth it.

As far as my mom; he cheated too much and she was over it. Hell yea, she took half of everything, like any woman would. We found out he had quite a few houses outta state, money in accounts overseas and a ton of women, he was taking care of. We were shocked to find out all the information, but

245

my mom was happy, she found out, sooner than later. He still has money but I guess since his son, is wealthier than him, he can't handle it. I wouldn't put it past him, if he's been working with Shanta, Cara or even Zaire, to try and take me out. I'm glad, I distanced myself from him and it was the best decision, I made.

"Whatever you did, I'm sure you caused but in the end, he is still your son and she's his mother. Don't you know, jealousy and envy, will get you killed." He laughed.

"By who? You? Honey, you don't have it in you, to kill a fly." Now Rakia, laughed, which made all of us look. Did my girl kill people in the last week, I don't know about, or better yet, is she planning it? I couldn't tell from her response.

"You're right. I am a little scary when it comes to killing anything but you see." She wiped her mouth and stood up. I saw her two bodyguards walking over.

"They're not." She pointed to them.

"These motherfuckers work for my son. They wouldn't dare lay hands on me." I grinned and so did Tech. We instilled in the girl's bodyguards, that if they wanted someone killed to do it, with no questions asked.

"They actually love me and will do anything I ask, so Mr. Santiago, I ask you again. Is it worth trying to hurt the mother of your son, or him?" My father looked at me and my mom, had a grin on her face.

"Marco, you're gonna let this bitch.-" Rakia tossed a drink in his face and Tech, told me to stay in my seat.

"I'ma fuck you up." He stood and Rak's two bodyguards, hemmed him up against the window. Tech, had a gun to his head and everyone in the restaurant, stopped to look.

"IF ANY OF YOU MOTHERFUCKERS TAKE A PHONE OUT, I'LL KILL YOU." I yelled. We didn't need this shit on YouTube, World star or any other social media sites. Nobody moved.

"You ungrateful niggas. After all I did, for you." Now it was my turn, to say something.

"You ok, baby?" She asked me.

"I'm good Rak. Tech, got me, if needed." He nodded. I kissed her lips and stood in front of my pops.

247

"I already let you slide for the shit, in the hospital. I was gonna let the guards take you outside and whoop your ass, for coming in here on some bullshit. Unfortunately, you fucked up by calling my woman a bitch. Now, its up to Rak, what she wants done to you. By the look on her face; I'd say, she isn't too happy and will probably wish death on you. And I must say pops, that since she's been in my life, I've never not, given her, exactly what she wants." I saw how terrified my pops was and so did Rak.

"Babe, whatever you wanna do, I'm fine with." I wanted her to be more specific.

"If you wanna feed him to sharks, its ok. Or, if you wanna kill him, by sticking a needle in his neck, full of poison, I'd be ok with that, too. What do you think ladies?" My mother and Ang, nodded in agreeance. I pulled her close.

"Damn, you sexy, barking out ways to kill him." She smiled and I heard Tech, suck his teeth. I don't know why, when he's the same with Ang.

"Welp! You heard her. Take him to the warehouse and we'll go from there." My pops was yelling and screaming obscenities throughout the restaurant. The people went back to eating and so did we. I'll deal with him later. I'm not about to let him ruin our dinner.

"I can't wait to fuck you later." I whispered in her ear.

"And, I can't wait for you to do it. Make sure you're well enough to be freaky. I miss that." She kissed my neck.

"You know, I'ma turn that pussy out." She smiled. I hope she knows, what she's asking, cuz a nigga ain't stopping, once I'm in it.

Rakia

"Mmmm, baby, I have to go." Marco continued kissing me at the door. Tonight, is my bachelorette party and the two of us, had sex most of the day.

"Don't get fucked up ma." He smacked me on the ass and opened the door. The driver was waiting for me. He refused to let me drive, until Zaire was found.

"You'll be the only one on my mind." I stuck my hand in his shorts and started to massaged his manhood.

"Keep it up, and you won't go nowhere." I removed my hand and pecked his lips, one more time.

"Don't let Brielle stay up late with you, either."

"Man, whatever. My daughter can stay up, as late as she wants." I waved him off and allowed the guard to shut the door. On the ride over, I checked my purse to make sure, what I needed was in there. I didn't really need one with this outfit, but being tonight will be one to remember, I wasn't taking any chances.

The guy parked the truck and my guards got out first to check the place out. Ang, came out to get me after seeing them, and I must say, I'm surprised Tech, let her ass out. Her shorts were small as hell, the shirt was covering her stomach but if she bent over you could see it and the bitch had Jordan's on. The shorts would look better in boots, in my opinion, but its her outfit.

She grabbed my hand and we walked in together. There were a few women there from the club, Tech owned. Missy was there, and so was Lizzie, my aunt Shanta, Cara and quite a few other women. You could also see guards posted up at every exit and a few on the walls. Marco, made sure no one would hurt me. The place was decorated beautifully, it was tons of food and drinks, and the DJ, was already playing music.

Throughout the night, I noticed Cara and Shanta, sitting at one of the tables together and not speaking to anyone. Both of them, had snarls on their faces but I refused to let them upset me. I didn't know why they would come, if this is what they planned on doing. Ang, asked why were they invited. I told her they wanted to make amends and I agreed for the sake of my grandmother. Of course, she said something was suspect and not to trust them and she's right. Cara, contacted me out of nowhere and wants to make amends, now. She absolutely, hates me for having a kid by Marco and being with him in general, which is why, all I talked about the day we went to eat, was him. I could see the aggravation on her face and all it did, was excite me and make me continue.

I kept my eye on them and also, met some of Marco's cousins, who came for the wedding. It was supposed to take place a few weeks ago, but with Tech, getting shot, then Marco, it had to be put on hold, but in another week, it would be all about me and I couldn't wait. I had to order a different dress and I must say, its more beautiful, than the original one, I had picked out. The shoes were especially designed for me, through the Prada website, thanks to Ang and his mom, ordered the veil. I planned on being the baddest bitch in the church.

"Hey, cousin in law." The chick Maria said. She was Marco's cousin, on his mother side. I loved her already because she was no nonsense and had me hysterical laughing, the entire time.

"What's up? You look aggravated." Missy and I, were sitting at one of the tables, waiting for the strippers, that Ang said, just arrived.

"I'm gonna end up hurting the bitch, who's supposed to be your aunt."

"Why? What happened?" She took a seat next to us.

"I overheard her saying, you think you're too good for them and they're about to take everything from you. Now, me being the bitch I am, asked what were they taking from you, and her voice disappeared. I mean, it could be the gun, I had to her temple." I covered my mouth laughing. I didn't even see the shit happen.

"The bitch in the wheelchair, attempted to talk shit and Leslie, cut it short." Leslie is her sister and I'm telling you, just meeting them tonight, told me they're nothing to fuck with.

"Ok, you two heffas. Its time to see the strippers." Lizzie said and we all turned around.

"Come here Ang and Maria." I asked them to step in a corner with me.

"What up?" I looked around and made sure no one was listening.

"I'm going to the bathroom and I want you to make sure, no one follows me."

"Umm, ok. What if the bitch and her aunt, try?" I smirked and walked away. Both of them, had a confused look on their face and I hoped, they understood because I damn sure didn't have time to explain. I went inside, used the stall and came out to wash my hands. I picked my phone up to call Marco. I desperately needed to hear his voice.

"Hey ma. You better not be allowing those steroid niggas to dance on you." I busted out laughing.

"No, baby. You're the only stripper, I want."

"I better be. What's up?"

"You trust me, right?"

"I do. What's wrong?"

"Hey Cara." I spoke, as she wheeled herself in the bathroom.

"CARA! Ma, please tell me she's not there." I ignored his question and asked about Brielle. She stared at me on the phone.

"I swear to God, Rak. Matter of fact, I'm on the way."

"Ok, but do me a favor and wait."

"I'm not waiting on shit. If I don't see you when I get there, I'm shutting everything down. Let me call Maria. I know she won't allow shit to happen and where's Ang?"

"Oh, they're watching the strippers but they know, I went to the bathroom. I'm about to go out there now. I was calling to check on Brielle."

"Pretend you're hanging up and leave me on the phone. I may be on the way, but I need to hear everything."

"Ok baby. Talk to you later." I left the phone on the counter, like he asked. I had the privacy screen on it, so you couldn't tell, if it were on, or not. I went in my purse and applied some lip-gloss.

"I guess, you had to check in with our man."

"I'm sorry but when did he become our man."

"Bitch. He's been our man." I shook my head. I knew she wouldn't change, which is the exact reason, I waited for her to come in here. Last time, her and Bobbi, harassed me and almost made me lose Brielle in a bathroom. It won't happen again, with this one in my stomach.

"Cara, I invited you here because you claimed, to want to make amends." She started laughing hysterically.

"Bitch, are you serious? I hate you and the ground you walk on."

"Well, tell me, how you really feel."

"Oh, I am." She wheeled herself closer to me and kept looking at the door. I wasn't worried because not only is my man on the way; Ang or Maria, won't allow anyone to come in here.

"You may have saw Marco first at the bodega, but I had him first." I waved her off.

"Cara, you sucked his dick and didn't do a good job, I might add." Marco told me she was horrible in the bedroom and couldn't suck dick. How about Tech, told Ang the same thing? I turned and looked in the mirror. The lip-gloss felt like it was on the side of my lip.

"I still had him first."

"Ok, he let you suck him off first, but we both know, I slept with him first." I gave her a fake smile.

"Are you really mad, he didn't want a woman who threw herself at him? A woman, who slept with his entire crew? A woman, who tried to kill his child's mother? A woman, who's been conspiring with Zaire, to kill both of us? I mean, why are you mad?" Her mouth fell open. She didn't think we knew the shit, she was into.

"Cara, I really wanted to believe you had good intentions on coming here to make amends. Unfortunately, I see you will never change." I grabbed my purse. Before I could turn around, she grabbed my leg and stabbed me with something.

"Ahhhhhh." I shouted and reached in my purse to get what I needed. She was able to get me again and the pain was excruciating. I could hear Marco, yelling through my phone.

"Fuck you bitch. I'm gonna make sure you can't have any more kids by him." She lifted both hands and attempted to stab me in the stomach.

CLICK! She froze and the knife fell out her hand. I had my gun on her forehead. Marco, brought me one, after he showed me how to shoot. I never thought, I'd need it but with a cousin like Cara, I'm glad he got it.

He and I, previously discussed him getting Cara and my aunt. It was no secret, he knew where they were but being the forgiving person I am, I kept asking him to wait; thinking they'll change. He asked, if I wanted to kill her and I told him no. However, after meeting her at my restaurant, I knew then; it needed to be me, to end her life.

I'm the one, she tormented for years. The one, she called retarded, weird, bitches and everything else, under the sun. She's the one, who attacked me before and if I didn't have this gun on her, she'd try and kill me now.

I felt the tears falling down my face. I wasn't crying because I'm about to kill her. I was crying because for years, I allowed her, to treat me like shit and I forgave her, over and over. I cried for the amount of pain, I was in. For the child, I may lose and for the only female cousin, I had. Then my aunt, turned on me, my mom and grandmother died and I finally figured out, in order for me to live free, she had to go. No if's, ands, or buts about it.

"I tried to love you Cara, but you are hateful and its time to rid myself of anyone, who's in my life, to cause pain."

"Please, don't kill me." I struggled to stand and wiped my eyes.

"I thought, you'd have a lot to say, when I had this gun on you. Unfortunately, nothing you say, nor any begging, is going to stop me from doing this."

"Don't do this Rakia. Grandma, wouldn't be happy." I had to laugh at her, trying to manipulate me into not taking her life. The nerve, after she literally, stabbed me twice.

PHEW! I shot her in the stomach. I wanted her to feel pain, before taking her life. She screamed and blood began pouring out. I felt no remorse and my hands were as calm, as ever.

PHEW! The second time, I shot her in the chest.

"I never wanted it to end this way Cara but if I didn't get you first, you'd kill me. Goodbye."

PHEW! The last bullet went straight through her forehead. I put the gun in my purse and fell to the ground. My leg was hurting bad and blood was seeping through my jeans. I slid over to the door, opened it up and there stood Ang and Maria. They helped me to a chair and I saw Lizzie coming towards me with a belt. I know, she isn't about to hit me. Instead, she wrapped it around my leg tightly. All of a sudden, the music stopped and everyone looked at the door. Marco, Tech, Doc and a few other dudes stood there. Someone pointed to me and he came rushing over.

"FUCK! Besides your leg, are you hurt anywhere else?"

"No. It hurts baby." He lifted me up.

"AHHHHHHHH. OH, MY GOD!" A woman screamed and my aunt came running out the bathroom.

"YOU FUCKING BITCH. YOU DID THIS." She pointed to me and everyone looked.

"Baby, she's gonna try and.-"

260

CLICK!

"I wish the fuck you would." Don't ask me where Ang, got her gun from but she surely had my back.

"And you thought, no one loved you." Tech went over to Ang and the other women went back to letting the dancers strip. I guess, this is normal, so they continued.

"She gonna be good?" Doc asked.

"Yea. Stay here with your wife. I'll call y'all when she sees the doctor." He closed the door. Two other trucks pulled off behind us.

"You ok?" He turned my face to his and wiped it with his sleeve.

"I had to do it. You think my grandmother is upset with me? What about Rahmel? He's gonna be mad. Marco.-" He kissed me to relax and like always, it worked.

"Rahmel told me a while ago, he was waiting for you to do it." My eyes got big.

"How you feel?"

"I don't know. I really thought you would kill her." He smiled.

"Trust me, when I say, we had eyes on her and your aunt. Rak, I wanted you to enjoy this week before our wedding. After our honeymoon, I was bringing you to the warehouse?"

"Why?"

"After all the shit, you've been through with them. Cara, deserved for you to be the one, taking her life." I nodded and laid my head back.

He carried me in the emergency room and they took me upstairs, right away. They checked the baby and he or she, is fine. I think we were both relieved to hear that. One of the stab wounds was really deep and I needed twenty stiches. The other one, she barely cut the skin.

In any case, I got four butterfly stitches on that one. They had me stay for two hours, just to monitor the baby's heartbeat and make sure, my pressure stayed normal. Once we left, we went home and his phone rang off the hook. Everyone was checking on me and Maria, wanted to know, what to do with Shanta. I told him, as of right now, I don't even care what they do with her. The person who I had to deal with, is gone and nothing else mattered. Well, of course, Zaire had to go, but

I'm sure, my future husband is gonna get him, when the time is right. He hung up and got in bed with me.

"You still walking down the aisle in a week?" He asked.

"I may limp but I wouldn't miss it for the world. Are you going to be standing there?" I threw the question on him.

"With motherfucking bells on baby. Nothing is gonna stop me from making you, Mrs. Santiago." He kissed me and put my leg on his. They told me to keep it elevated. He was making sure of it, too. I dosed off, thinking of how I couldn't wait to meet him, at the altar, on our wedding day. It took a lot getting here and I feel like him. No one is going to stop the show. NO ONE!

Rahmel

"I'm glad she killed her." I looked over at Missy in the car. We had just left the bachelorette party Marco's mom, threw for Rak. After he took her to the hospital, all of the guys stayed and made sure Cara was disposed of properly. My mother cried the entire time and I finally made her leave because Marco's mom, cousin and even Ang, wanted to murder her. It wasn't to protect her either. I planned on asking Rak what she wanted to do as far as, my mom goes. I know y'all think I'm crazy but I've seen too much to worry about her fate. When I said, I no longer had a mother or sister, I meant it. This is actually my first time seeing them, since Cara called the cops on Rak, for tossing her out the wheelchair, which was funny as hell, I might add. I almost peed on myself from laughing so hard. When I told my girl, she did the same thing.

"Mannnnnn. It's been a long time coming." I rubbed my hair on the top of my head.

Not too long ago, I ran into Marco and Tech, at the club. I had just walked in and someone came straight to me and had me go to VIP. One of the guys from the garage came with me, so I asked if it were ok for him to come in. I never expected any favors from Marco just because he dated my cousin. Shit, it didn't bother me to lay low, or not have the kind of money he did. As long as my girl and daughter were good, it's the only thing that mattered.

When we stepped in, I spoke and gave both of them, the man hug and took a seat. The guy with me, seemed to be nervous as hell. He was more or less a geek but well aware of who Marco and Tech were. I had to tell him to relax, just to get him to take a drink. These two, definitely instilled fear in everyone but the way I see it is, if you stayed outta their way, you had nothing to worry about. As usual, you had the niggas who always tested you, but overall, they didn't really beef with anyone, that I know of.

Anyway, Marco asked if I'd be mad, if he killed Cara? Not that he cared but I respected him for asking; even though it was more for Rakia. We all knew, she wouldn't dare confront my sister, or mother for that matter. However, I tried to tell them on plenty of occasions to leave Rak alone, but they never listened. I guess, they thought Marco was only fucking my cousin but that was far from the truth. Since meeting her, he's purchased her cars, businesses, gave her money, a child, with one on the way, is getting ready to marry her and would kill anyone who fucked with her; family or not. My cousin had him, wrapped around her finger and everyone knew it.

Long story short, I told him to be my guest. I did tell him that maybe he should, teach her how to use a gun, just in case he couldn't get to her in time and look. Push came to shove and Rak, did what she had to. I thought she'd be a little more shaken up but after all she's been through. I guess getting her out the way, is something that's been a long time coming. Now, I'm sure my mother is gonna come full throttle at her, for taking her precious Cara away. I hope she's ready for what he'll do because, he's gonna do a lot worse than Rak.

"She really hated Rak."

"And you know, my cousin has always been loyal to her. Rak, would do anything for Cara, or anyone else who needed something. My sister became worse once Marco came in the picture. She was obsessed with him and he wanted

266

nothing to do with her. Shit, I'm embarrassed for the way she acted."

"I thought your mom loved Rak."

"She did until Cara started with her bullshit. It was like she became so blinded by my sisters lies, she forgot about loving Rak. She knew my cousin looked up to her as a mother figure and still shitted on her." Missy shook her head.

"I'll never treat our daughter like that, or this one." She rubbed her belly. Yea, I fucked around and got her pregnant again. Missy, is gonna be my wife. At first, I debated about marriage but seeing how happy Tech is and how Marco, can't wait to marry Rakia, makes me wanna be just as happy. Call me corny but my kids will grow up in a two-parent household.

I had a good job, brought a house for us, we both had brand new cars and my bank account is lovely, thanks to Rak. When my grandmother died, she had an insurance policy for over a million dollars. She left it to Rak, who gave it to me. I tried to fight her on it but she wouldn't allow me too. I even asked Marco to make her keep it but he said, he's fighting her to keep the money, he put in her account. My cousin has a good heart and it's the reason, I protected her from Cara, as much as, possible.

"I'm not worried about that. You're an excellent mom and if you weren't, I wouldn't dare put another one in you." She leaned over and kissed me, when we pulled in the driveway.

"You know we never had sex outside." She smirked and lifted the shirt over her head.

"Nothing like the present, to do it." I moved my seat back and helped her get comfortable on top of me. I unsnapped her bra, put one of her breasts in my mouth and caressed the other one.

"Mmmmm." She moaned out and I could feel her hands on my jeans. Once she undid them, and moved my boxers down, she mounted me. I had to moan out myself, from how good her pussy gripped my dick.

"Fuck Missy. Ride that shit." I smacked her on the ass and watched her go faster.

"I'm cumming Rahmel."

"Me too. Shitttttttt." We aggressively kissed one another and moaned in each other's mouth, as we came. Ain't nothing like a quickie, before the real deal.

"I love you Rahmel." She stared in my eyes.

"I love you too. What's up?"

"With everything going on, I wanna make sure you know."

"Let's go in, so I can tear that ass up." She laughed and opened the car door. She stepped out and gasped.

"You scared me." I hopped out quick as hell, only to come face to face, with my mother.

"I guess you fucked her nasty ass in the car."

"Bitch, I'll fuck you up out here." Missy put her shirt on and I pushed her behind me. There's no way, I'd allow my mother to put hands on my girl, pregnant or not.

"Go inside and check on my daughter. Be ready for me." Her mom had my daughter. She came to visit and stayed for the weekend. She was cool as hell and I wished, mine was the same. I leaned down to kiss her and my mom sucked her teeth. I shut the car door and leaned on it. There's no need for her to come in.

"Why are you here?"

"Rahmel, Rakia killed your sister and you're acting non chalant about it."

"It's because I don't care." I headed to my door.

"How could you say that? Would you be this less caring, if she killed your ugly ass girlfriend?" I yoked her up by the shirt.

"First off... my girl ain't nowhere near ugly. Second... Rakia loves my girl, like her sister so I won't ever worry about shit happening to her. You're sitting here pretending, Cara didn't harass Rak, her entire life. You of all people, knew how Cara was. Shit, it's the reason I left. You're so worried about your daughter but how many times did you try and get me to come home?" She didn't say a word.

"EXACTLY!! I was your son and you allowed me to go on my own, at the age of seventeen. Not once did you even extend a helping hand, in getting me a place. I stayed with my grandparents and Rak. It may not have been far but it felt more like home, than the place you raised me in."

"But she was your sister."

"And you were my mother." She wiped the tears. I don't doubt she's upset about Cara, but she knew it was coming.

"I told you a long time ago, to set your daughter straight but you let her do and say whatever she wanted to people. You're lucky Rak, got her and not all the other enemies, she has out there."

"Rahmel?" Missy opened the door for me.

"Yea babe."

"When you're finished, can you run to McDonalds and grab me, two large fries?" She smiled and I laughed. This pregnancy had her craving those fries, damn near everyday.

"Bitch, don't you see us talking?" I couldn't hold my girl back, any longer. My mom had disrespected her too many times and she deserved an ass whooping.

"What is going on?" Missy's mom came out and tried to stop her.

"Nah, ma. I got this." Yea, I called her ma. Missy and I, have been together for four years and she was more like a mother to me, then my own.

"I'm tired of you bitch." My mother yelled out, after I finally pulled Missy off her. I yelled at her for fighting pregnant. Shanta, deserved the shit and I prayed she didn't lose it. I noticed my mom pull a gun out and that was it. I wrestled her to the ground and I could hear Missy, yelling for me to stop.

BOOM! Is all you heard in the distance.

"OH MY GOD! RAHMEL, ARE YOU OK?" I heard Missy and stood up. I stared down into the eyes of my mother, who was gasping for air. Blood was coming out her mouth as the bullet to her stomach, began killing her.

"What are we gonna do? The noise was loud. What if someone calls the cops?"

"Go in the house. I'll handle it."

"But Rahmel."

"Ma. Take her inside please." I waited for her to close the door and let a few tears drop, for my real mother. If only she had the ability to love her kids the right way, none of this would be happening. I did the only thing, I could in a situation like this. I picked my phone up and dialed a number.

"Yo!" He sounded half sleep.

"Can you swing through? Its an emergency."

"You good?"

"Yea, my mom came by and.-"

"Say no more." I hung up and waited. Hopefully, they'll get here before the cops, if they were even called. Our neighborhood is pretty secluded but it doesn't mean, no one heard the shot. Maybe, they'll think its something else because I'll have a hard time explaining this.

Marco

"It better be an emergency. Ang was about to ride the shit outta me." I hung the phone up on his stupid ass. Tech knows, I hate when he speaks of their sex life. Another bitch yea, but Ang, no. She's like my damn sister so its disgusting to me. My phone rang back.

"Yo, I'm about to stop fucking with you." I threw on a pair of jeans, a hoodie and some Jordan's.

"Yea, fucking right." I had to laugh because he knew, that shit would never happen.

"What the hell you want? How's Rak?"

"She good. The doctor gave her something to help her with the pain and it put her to sleep. But I called because I think Rahmel and his mom, had it out."

"I'm on my way. What's his address again?" I gave it to him and grabbed my things to leave. I kissed Rak, on the forehead and did the same with Brielle.

Once I got in the car, I lit a black and mild. Rahmel never calls me unless it has to do with Rak. I assumed him and his mom had it out, because he showed up at the bachelorette party too. I'm sure she had words about him not being upset, Cara was dead. Shanta wanted everyone to feel bad but she was the only one. Hell, Rak's father called her at the hospital and said he heard from Shanta, what went down. He told her good job and that her grandfather and him, were proud of her, for finally standing up for herself. I made sure she cut the conversation short because we damn sure didn't need him asking too much. She could tell both of them in person.

I pulled up to his house at the same time Tech did and parked behind his car. There was a woman laid out in the grass and if you looked on the ground, there was a trail of blood going down the driveway. Missy was hugging his waist and I guess her mom, was at the door with the baby. Now, from the looks of things, one of them killed Shanta. Tech, started laughing and fired up a blunt. We damn sure would need it, listening to this shit.

I stepped around her, so the blood didn't get on my new Jordan's and asked what happened. Missy walked up and gave Tech and I, a hug and went in the house. She was growing on

275

us, especially; now that the girls took her, under their wing. She was cool, so it didn't bother me, plus she'll be Rak's cousin in law, soon.

"Soooooooo, you couldn't take her shit no more, huh?"

"No, that's not it, even though it's the truth. She came over, wondering why I could care less about Cara dying. Her and my girl got into it. Missy beat her ass and my mom pulled a gun on her. I tackled her to the ground, the gun went off and there you have it. A deadbeat mom, in the middle of my driveway." Tech and I, looked at each other.

"I know its expensive to get someone out here and I'll pay you everything in my bank account. I just don't wanna go to jail. Missy's pregnant again and I wanna make sure we walk down the aisle and.-"

"Bro, really?" Tech asked and I shook my head.

"What?"

"You can tell you're related to Rakia. You ramble when you're nervous, too." I told him.

"Mannnnn. Y'all know, I'm not a street nigga. I may fuck with them but I don't know what to do, in a situation like this."

I stood there listening to him and could tell he was nervous and had a good heart too. All he wanted was his mother to love him, the right way and the same with Cara. Rak, told me about the many times he protected her from Cara, so of course, I'd have his back right now. I admit, it was funny as hell, watching him sweat and Tech, thought so too, which is why he kept telling him, the cops would come and put the light in the driveway and find blood. This nigga, was damn near about to pack his family up and bounce.

"Tech, stop fucking with him. He nervous as shit." He couldn't stop laughing.

"First off... my wife." Yea, in a week, she'll be Mrs. Santiago, so I may as well get used to saying it.

"My wife would kick my ass, if I didn't help you. Second... Go in the house and don't come out until the morning."

"But what about all this?"

277

"Don't ask questions. Tomorrow is a new day and you'll never have to worry about anything that happened here tonight."

"Are you gonna help him Marco?" Missy was at the door, just as nervous as he was.

"Goodnight, you two." Rahmel stared at his mother, one more time and took Missy in the house. I heard the doors lock and all the downstairs lights went out and the ones upstairs, clicked on.

"You should've let me fuck with him, some more."

"He was about to shit on himself and you know damn well, Missy would've been on the phone with Ang, first thing in the morning and you would've gotten an earful."

"What the fuck ever? Ang, don't run this." I looked at him and we both started laughing. Shit, our women have us on lock and we couldn't deny it, if we wanted to.

About ten minutes later, my peoples came to clean the mess up in Rahmel's driveway. I let them know, their accounts were filled as they cleaned up. I sent it over the phone, as a bank transfer, like I did anyone working for me. Its always good to make sure your employees are paid well and in a timely manner. That way, they'll always be there for you, when you really need them. I dapped Tech up and we both headed home. I locked the door, put the alarm on and got in the bed.

"Did he kill her?" I heard Rakia say.

"Who?"

"Rahmel. Baby, I heard his voice when you answered the phone."

"I thought you were sleep and why was your nosy ass listening?"

"I was dosing off and anytime your phone rings, I can listen, if I want to."

"You're right. You can ride this dick if you want to, too." She sucked her teeth and rolled over.

"Ahhhh, shit." She yelled out when she accidently laid on her leg.

"That's what your smart ass gets." I mushed her in the head and she elbowed me in the side.

"Ma, look at me." She rolled over.

"He did what he had to, to protect his girl."

"You better not let him go to jail."

"Don't insult me."

"MARCO!"

"I didn't ma, damn."

"I was gonna say, if he spent one second in there, your ass would be on pussy punishment for a very long time."

"Yea, fucking right. That pussy craves this dick, as much as this dick, craves her."

"You make me sick." She snickered and laid on my chest.

"I'll never let anyone you love go to jail. Now, those dead motherfuckers didn't deserve jail either, which is why, they are where they are."

"I love you so much baby." She lifted her head to kiss me.

"You better. I ain't putting my seeds in you, or giving you my last name because you're obsessed over me."

"I can't stand you. Goodnight." She went on her side of the bed and I slid her closer to me.

"You know, I need you right here, when we sleep. There's no space in between."

"Now who's spoiled?"

"You damn right. I told you Rak, you're my favorite blanket and I need you around at all times." I felt something wet on my arm.

"Save the crying for when you see this sexy nigga, standing at the altar waiting for you." She busted out laughing but a nigga was serious. Shit, my tux is the shit.

"You are a mess. Goodnight."

"Goodnight ma."

****

Wedding Day...

"Come the fuck on, bro. Shit, I don't wanna hear my wife's mouth because yo ass, late." Tech shouted and Doc, sat in the backseat laughing. Today is my wedding day and I had to handle something before even going to the church.

Rak, told me not to call her today, so last night, I stayed on the phone with her for an hour, and once it hit 11:59, she told me, to see her at the altar. I was mad because she wasn't asleep next to me and I couldn't speak to her, until later.

"I'm coming damn." I closed the door and put my head back. Today is already turning out good. All I needed to do is get to the church by 4pm. I looked down at my phone and it was already 2:30. We had to be in and out.

Tech, parked around the corner and the two truckloads of guys we came with, were behind us. We all got out the car, ready for war. We all had on black, our vests were on, and since it was raining, no one was outside. I'm sure Rak, isn't happy about the rain but it's supposed to clear up in an hour. I hope it does because I don't wanna hear her mouth.

Each of us, scoped out the scenery and I stepped on the porch. You could hear mad people inside and music playing. Who the hell, is on the run and out here living it up, or should I say, not being discreet?

"On the count of three." They all nodded.

"One... Two... THREE..." I shouted and kicked the door in, to Rakia's grandparents' house. See when Shanta died, Rahmel and Missy, went to the house to clean it out. If anything happened to them, it automatically, went to him. He planned on renting it out and using it for income. Like I said before, he may not be a street nigga but he's a hustla, for sure.

Anyway, the day they came, there were a few men on the porch. Since no one knew who he was, he asked who's house it was because it was for rent, in the paper. One of the guys told him, their boy from Connecticut called them down. I asked if he knew a name and he said, no but they were here to settle a score with some dude. It made me think of the chick Mary, we still had in the warehouse. I went there and had her contact her brother, tell him she was good and ask who were the dudes, that came.

Once he told her, they came for Zaire and it was some, up and coming hustlers who didn't know any better, I knew the time to strike was now. After she made the call, I gave her a bus ticket back to Connecticut and told her if she ran her mouth to anyone, I would feed her to my dog. She promised not to and sat at the bus stop until one came. I made sure someone kept an eye on her, and even had a few people watching her in Connecticut for a while. I didn't trust anyone. Now back to this idiot.

"Well, well, well. What do we have here?" There were niggas on the couch playing a video game, some in the kitchen smoking, others on the back porch and you could hear moaning upstairs.

"Who the fuck are you?"

PHEW! Tech laid his ass out and Doc, cussed him out because he wanted to take the first life.

"Down goes Frazier." I yelled and no one moved.

"Where is Zaire?" None of them said a word. I nodded and four more bodies dropped.

"SHIT! He upstairs. What the fuck?" This kid didn't look to be any older than 16.

"Who are you?" I stood in his face.

"Ummmm. Robert. I'm here with my brother. Please don't kill me. I don't even know why he came. I told him not to be bothered with Zaire. He's nothing but trouble."

"Who's your brother?" He didn't wanna tell me and even with the gun on his forehead, he still refused.

"You got heart little nigga. I like that. Too bad you're on the wrong team."

"WAIT!" He yelled out.

"I have information, if you promise not to kill me or my brother."

"What about these last few?" He shrugged his shoulders.

"I don't know any of them. I just want me and my brother, to make it home to my mom."

"Depending on the info, we'll see."

"Zaire has a grenade, bomb or something and said he was gonna use it at some guys' wedding. If you don't believe me, look in his car out front." One of the guys ran outside. The crazy part is, the music was turned down and yet, this nigga hadn't emerged from the room. I spoke into the walkie talkie. Hell yea, we were on some cop shit.

"Keep an eye on all the exits and the minute you see him, shoot or bring him to me." Everyone said ok.

285

"Yooooo, this is some powerful shit." One of the guys said. He walked in with a big ass box, with a timer on it, that wasn't started yet and it definitely looked like, it could blow up a lotta shit.

"Good looking out, my nigga." I gave him a dap and let him and his brother leave.

"Robert." He turned around and I could see the look of fear on him and his brothers face.

"Yea."

"I suggest you to go home and thank God for saving you. Had you lied, you'd be dead with the rest of these niggas." And just like that, we made sure the rest of their bodies dropped in front of them.

"Oh, Roberts brother." He swallowed hard.

"Don't ever follow behind a nigga, you know nothing about. As you can see, the shit will get you killed." He nodded.

"Take your ass to Connecticut and never return. And to make sure you don't, someone will have their eyes on you for a very long time. Be easy now." They left and one of the guys said, they ran to their car.

"Let's get rid of this nigga." I slowly walked up the steps and still heard moaning. I kicked the door open and some chick was riding him. I looked harder and it was the nurse bitch who disrespected my wife, when I was shot. Yea, we used to fuck but that was it and like Tech said, everyone knew about Rak, so she knew exactly what she was doing.

"Marco?" It took me all of two seconds, to shoot her in between the eyes. Zaire, tossed her body and tried to reach for the gun on the nightstand. How the hell is he sleeping with another bitch, in Rak's old room.

"We meet again and this time, no one's here to get in my way." I was pissed in Connecticut when I tried to kill him. People started running and screaming and I lost sight of his dumb ass.

"So, you're just gonna kill me, instead of fighting me like a man." We all tossed our heads back laughing.

"Fight you like a man, huh?" I took my vest off, handed my gun to Tech and cracked my neck.

"What time is it?"

"3:15." I had to hurry up. All of us, had to get dressed and be at the church. He stood and tried to square up.

"You're out your rabid ass mind, if you think, I'm gonna beat your ass with no clothes on." He hurried to get dressed and the minute he looked at me, I stole his ass. He was dazed like a motherfucker.

"You didn't give me a chance to.-" I hit his ass again in the ribs. He hunched over in pain.

"Nigga, I ain't with the talking shit." I continued beating his ass, until he was damn near passed out.

"You finished, or you want more?" He couldn't respond because half his teeth were on the ground.

"Bro, its getting late." Tech yelled. I asked him for my gun.

"Say hello to your mother and brother?"

PHEW! PHEW! PHEW! I made sure his ass was dead. We didn't need him coming back, talking about you forgot to kill me.

"Bring me the bomb." Doc ran downstairs to get it.

"You really about to set the shit off?"

288

"Yup. It's a lot of bodies in here. At least with the explosion, everything will be ashes."

"Smart!"

"I know Doc."

"What the fuck ever?" He waved me off and told everyone to get out the house. I flipped the switch on the side and saw the timer click on. We literally had 50 seconds to get the fuck out. Both of us, took off and ran to the truck. All of us, stood there waiting and it seemed like more than a minute passed. I glanced at the phone a few minutes later and sure enough, another three passed.

"Yo, are you serious? The shit didn't even work." We all started laughing and outta nowhere, the entire house exploded. The fucking ground shook and debris was everywhere.

"I bet it said five minutes, didn't it?" Tech asked and I shrugged my shoulders. It could have, since I was in a rush to get outta there, I didn't pay close attention. I made a call to the captain of the police station and told him, to make sure, to say it was a gas leak and to leave it at that. He agreed and I hopped in the truck. I wasn't worried because the fire chief, is on my payroll too.

All of us drove to the hotel and went in our separate rooms to get ready. After I stepped out the shower and put my clothes on, there was a knock at the door. My phone went off at the same time. It was a message from the fire chief saying he got the message, from the captain and he'll send me the report to show proof, it was only a gas leak. I responded with ok, and once I see it, he'll have a nice lump sum.

"Hey." Rakia's father and grandfather spoke. I let them in and went to grab my shoes.

"What up?" I sat down and put them on.

"We're just here to say, thank you for everything you've done for Rakia and it's unfortunate, her grandmother couldn't be here, but I know she's smiling down." Her grandfather said and gave me a hug. I didn't get to respond because her pops spoke.

"I haven't been the best parent, I know, but seeing my daughter happy, is all I ever wanted. I don't ever want you to stop treating her like the queen she is. Rakia, has been through a lot, as you know and she depends on you to love and cherish her." I smiled because she mentioned it to me before.

"She's fragile and she loves hard, which is why, it was hard for her, to allow anyone to bring harm to Cara and Shanta. Thanks for coming into her life and taking care of her." He gave me a hug.

"Just so you know, there will never be a time, where you have to worry about her." Tech walked in with Doc and Rahmel, came in before the door closed.

"Rakia, my daughter and all my future kids will always be protected, every time they leave the house. They are always my main concern, no matter where I'm at." Both of them nodded and told me, they'd see me at the church.

"You had your fatherly talk, with your in laws?" Tech, was always being a damn comedian.

"Shut yo ass up. Bring me my shot." Rahmel came over with a bottle of Henney and four glasses. He filled them up and we all, took it to the head.

"Whewwwww! Let me get my ass to the church. Its 4:15 and Ang, hit my line five times already, asking why we're not there."

"Shit, she cursed me the fuck out, for not getting you there in time but get this." We all looked at him.

"I asked if Rak was ready and were they, there. She had the nerve to tell me no, but that's not the point."

"That's your wife." We all walked out and headed out the door. The Rolls Royce limo was outside waiting. Even though the kid informed me of the bomb, I still had my guards run a thorough check under it. I'm getting married today, no matter what it takes.

"You ready to be tied down?" Tech asked.

"Never been more ready, about anything in my life."

"So, you're marrying her?" I heard and turned around.

"What the fuck you want, Ms. Connie and how the hell, did you know I was here?"

"Ever since you took Mia away, I've been a mess. Her son won't stop crying and.-" I put my hand up.

"Its your fault, for fucking with my girl. I never had plans on doing it, but once you approached my woman and said some bullshit, you signed her death certificate."

The day she spoke that bullshit to Rak in the nail salon, I went straight to the hospital, and smothered Mia to death. She may have been my first love but she lost any sympathy or compassion, I had for her, when she slept and stayed with Dennis. I messed up and fucked her, my girl left me, took forever to take me back and I made sure, she wouldn't bother her ever again.

"Nana." I heard. Tech and I, both looked and the kid was a spitting image of Dennis. I just shook my head and got in the limo. This bitch really thought showing me, the kid, would make me change my mind and give her money. She's a dumb bitch.

"Let's roll." I told the driver and he pulled off to take me, to meet my future wife at the altar.

We got out the limo and there were a few guards at the door and Tech told me, Ang text and said they were on the way. I made my way down the aisle, with my brother on the side of

293

me. Doc and a few of the other guys had to wait because they were walking down the aisle with some of the bridesmaids. I stood there for a good ten minutes, when the doors opened. I saw people looking, as the song *All My Life* played by KC and JoJo. I don't care how many people used this song. The words they spoke are exactly, how I felt about her

Missy and Rahmel came down first, Doc and his wife came second, the rest of the wedding party came after. My nephew, lil Tech as I call him, walked with the rings on a pillow. The women were loving him and he was eating the shit up. For him to be two, he knew the game already. I told Ang, he was gonna be a ho but she don't believe me.

My mom walked down with Rakia's grandfather, who had Brielle, in his other arm. She was grabbing him tight, looking at all the people. She was my damn twin and spoiled as hell. Soon as she saw me, she wouldn't stop crying and reached out for me. I had him, hand her to me and we both stood, waiting for her mom. The doors closed again and reopened. Another song played and I heard, people saying *Wow,* and *She's gorgeous.*

When Rakia came in my view, I had to do a double take. She was more beautiful than I've ever seen and that's hard because she's gorgeous. Her dress had rhinestones or some shit around the top area and the bottom was flared out, with a long ass train behind it. The veil covered her face but I could still tell she was crying. I know she wanted a Cinderella wedding, and its exactly what she got. I handed Brielle to her favorite uncle and watched my future, finish coming down the long ass aisle. *DAMN! She was beautiful.*

Rakia

"Are they there yet? What if Marco changed his mind? It would be embarrassing to tell everyone there's no wedding."

"Girl, hush up. That nigga ain't missing the wedding." His cousin Maria said and finished putting my makeup on. Ang, told me she spoke to Tech and they were on their way. It was late and I was surprised because the bride is the only one, who's supposed to keep guests waiting. Granted, I'm going to be late but he should've been standing there.

"Ok, turn around." I did what she said and all the women, smiled.

"You look beautiful Rak and my son, is going to cry." Lizzie kissed my cheek and placed the veil on my head.

"You think so? I hope he likes the dress. My stomach is poking out a little and.-"

"RAKIA!" They all shouted.

"Calm your ass down. Damn! He loves you, in anything you wear." Ang said and bent down to slide, my shoes on my feet. I could get used to the pampering.

Today was my day and I'm nervous; yet, excited to become Mrs. Santiago. I stood up and the girls, all began taking pictures. I made sure to ask them not to post, in case someone was there and showed him. I wanted to witness his face, as he saw me. His mom pulled me to the side.

"Rakia, I want you to have these." She handed me a huge pair of diamond stud earrings.

"I can't take those." She pushed the veil back and put them in my ear, anyway. I didn't plan on wearing any earrings but she changed that.

"WOW! Those are beautiful." Ang's Mom said and gave me a hug. There was a knock at the door.

"Ladies, your limo awaits." Lizzie's boyfriend said. He was so nice and I love how they loved on each other. But then again, I love to see everyone in love.

"It's time." Ang grabbed both of my hands and stood directly in front of me.

"Rak, I know we had our issues during high school but I'm so happy you're my best friend and sister. You've gone through so much and deserve this day more than anyone. I'm so happy for you." She hugged me and I had to dab my eyes, to keep the tears from falling.

"Thanks for becoming my friend. You've been there through everything with Marco and I truly appreciate it. You didn't change up around Cara and it really showed, you were down for me. There's no one else, I wanted as my Matron of Honor, but you." She started crying and Lizzie told us to talk about it later.

On the ride to the church my stomach was in knots. The girls were taking more flicks and getting super excited too. His mom kept staring and smiling at me. I wanted so badly to call Marco and let him relax me but I told him not to speak to me, until I got to the altar. What the hell was I thinking?

The car stopped in front of the church and a woman came down and opened the door. She introduced herself as the wedding planner. All of us, looked at each other. Being this was a pretty quick wedding, I never hired one and we did all the decorations last night, ourselves. Maria, was about to go in on her but Lizzie pulled her to the side and said something.

The smile on her face, told me she was up to something. The groomsmen, all gave me a hug and took their places, with the ladies, to walk down the aisle.

"Ms. Winters, welcome to your enchanted wedding." The woman said and opened the doors.

"OH MY GOD!" I cried out. I could see inside but made sure not to let anyone see me yet.

The entire church was decorated in silver, baby blue and a streak of lavender, here and there. There was a white rug, leading into the church with silver confetti, all over it. There were balloons, streamers and four cages, with 2 white doves in them, hanging over the guests. What really amazed me, were the four women dressed as angels, in four areas of the church. Two, had a big harp in front of them, and the other two, had violins. How in the hell, did he do this, without me knowing?

"When... did he do this? I can't right now..." I was about to cry.

"Get it together love. He's giving you the wedding of your dreams. You wanted a Cinderella theme and that's what you got. Enjoy it because this is just the beginning." The woman said.

I got myself ready to walk down the aisle and started thinking about, how I had absolutely no friends growing up, and now, it seems like I had more than, I can handle. Ang and Missy, have become my sisters. Maria, Leslie and Doc's wife are growing on me. They are super ghetto, loud and will fight anyone over me. I have to get used to being around them.

I heard music being played. The women with the harps and violins, played a song, that sounded like *Fortunate*, by Maxwell. I looked up and he was standing there, singing it. Marco, went all out for me and I'm gonna make sure, he gets rewarded well, for it.

With each step I took, my body started to shake. My father, patted my arm in a way to get me calm. People were staring, taking pictures and recording. All I wanted to do, is say I do, and go on my honeymoon. The moment Marco locked eyes with me, the tears fell on their own. He smiled, which always made my heart melt. I got to the front and my dad placed my hand in Marco's and waited for the reverend to ask, who gave me away. Once he walked away the ceremony started. He asked if we had our own vows and I wasn't sure if Marco had written anything because we never spoke about it, but when he said yes, I was shocked.

"Rakia Winters, you are the only woman in this world, who wouldn't take my shit. Oh shit, we not supposed to cuss. My bad reverend." Everybody started laughing.

"You're the only woman who wouldn't take my mess. The woman, who told me no and meant it. The woman, who made me work for her love and her heart. The woman, who went out of character, just to show me she was down. And the woman, who stole my heart." Tears started falling so fast, I tried to wipe them but they wouldn't stop.

"Rakia Winters, you are my backbone and my rock. Before you, marriage was never, ever, in my future; yet, one look at you and I knew you would be the one, who changed my philosophy. Ma, I told you before, you're my favorite blanket but I left out, you being, the best thing that's ever happened to me. You gave me a daughter and are about to bless me with more kids. I could never repay you for it but I promise to be faithful. I promise, to listen when you need to talk. I promise, to work out any issues we come across. And last but not least, I promise to love you, until my last breath and even then, I'll love you in spirit. Rak, I'm so in love with you and I'm telling you in front of all these people, there's no leaving me. You're stuck for life." He pulled my face to his and kissed me.

"WOW!" The reverend said and I turned around to see a lot of women, with tears eyes.

"Ummmm, baby, I'm not sure, I can top that."

"Try. If you can, I'll buy you a house where ever you want." The audience chuckled.

"Where do I start?" I blew my breath in the air and wiped the rest of my tears.

"Marco Santiago, the first day, I laid eyes on you, I fell in love, without even knowing your name, or if you were in a situation." He smiled, like he always does, when I mention that.

"It wasn't until over a year later, that we'd run into one another again and from there, you've been a fixture in my life, good or bad."

"Yup." He was always so sure if himself.

302

"The night you asked me to be your girl, I was the happiest person in the world. You don't know this but I ran in the bathroom when you were asleep, shut the door and jumped up and down because I was so happy. Out of all the women in the world, you chose me and it meant a lot because I was always the outcast in school and on the streets. People called me a weirdo, slow, retarded and the list goes on and on. I guess, when you've heard it for so many years, you start to believe it." He turned his face up. Marco, never liked when I spoke on, how hard it was for me growing up. He always says, he wishes, he knew me sooner, so he could protect me from it.

"But not you. From the very start, you loved everything about me. The way, I stutter when I'm excited, and ramble on, when I'm nervous. You loved me anyway. Throughout, all the nonsense I've encountered, you never left me. And God knows, I thought it would be too much and you'd wake up and say, I'm not worth it." I felt the tears falling down my face again. He used his hands to wipe them away.

"I used to run away because I was scared and tried to please everyone, in bad situations, until you told me, every

303

person isn't worth forgiving." He asked someone for a tissue and handed it to me.

"When it came to me, you've told me over and over, I'm worth saving and honestly, I didn't think I was. Marco, you taught me how to love, how to stand up for myself, how to use my voice, how to protect my family and how to see my worth." I grabbed his hands.

"Baby, you are my best friend, my lover, my heart and my King. I love the way, you love me. I love, how you try and keep me from getting upset over the small things. I love how you make love to me. I love everything about you and I'm happy you chose me to spend the rest of your life with. I'm happy, you felt this weirdo, was worth the time and effort you put in, to get me. I promise, to keep you happy in every way. I promise, to give you all my time and attention, if you need it. I promise, not to run away, when times get hard and I promise, to stay in love with you, even in death. Marco Santiago, you will never be alone again, as long as I'm alive. I will love you, to my last breath and you're stuck with me too." I wiped the few tears that came down his face.

"How did I do?"

"Ma, I'll buy you a house in every state and country, if you want." We started kissing and we didn't stop, until we were pulled away. The reverend asked for the rings and once he finished talking and announced us, husband and wife, we went back to kissing.

"Alright damn." Tech and Doc, yelled at the same time.

"Can we get to the reception, I'm hungry?" Ang asked and my husband, mushed her in the head. We turned to walk out and people were congratulating us and asking for hugs, left and right. It took us a few minutes to get out the church.

"Marco, you didn't!" There was a horse and carriage outside.

"Isn't that how Cinderella left the church?" He took my hand in his and we ran under the people throwing rice.

"I can't believe you did all this for me."

"Rak, if you don't know by now, I'll do anything for you." The ride over to the reception was fun. The guy strolled through the park and once we went on the streets, people were waving and taking pictures.

"Marco."

"Yea." He turned to look at me.

"What's up?"

"I have a surprise for you." I pulled the paper out the bouquet. I stuck it in there so I wouldn't lose it. He opened it up and gave me a confusing look.

"Rak, I've already seen one of these." He spoke of the ultrasound photo, I put in his hands.

"I know and we promised not to find out the sex of the baby, until we deliver. However, when you went to the bathroom, the night Cara, stabbed me, I asked the doctor what we were having."

"Don't tell me, I'm having a son." We assumed this one was a girl too because I had the same morning sickness, I had with Brielle.

"There's your son." He looked back at the photo and then me.

"I FUCKING LOVE YOU RAKIA SANTIAGO!" He asked the guy to stop and pull the top over the carriage. The side doors covered our bodies and there was a small window. I'm telling you, the carriage was just like Cinderella's.

"Get your husband right, before we get to the reception." He unbuttoned his pants and pulled my other best friend out. I licked my lips, lifted my dress and climbed on top of him.

"You know people can see us." I told him and moved in circles.

"You wanna stop?" He held me still. I looked around.

"Nahhhhhh. This spontaneous sex, is fun. Now let me finish consummating this marriage.

"Hell yea ma. This pussy got me strung the fuck out."

"Really!" I always got excited when he told me, how well, I pleased him.

"Yea Rak. Fuck me harder." I popped down harder. The carriage stopped but we didn't. Marco asked, the guy to park it in the back and give us some privacy. We went at it for a while, in that damn carriage. Both of us were moaning out each other's name. By the time we finished, his phone was ringing off the hook.

"We coming in now."

"Marco, I have cum all over my legs."

"Let me see." I lifted my dress and my husband literally, licked me dry and that's after he pulled a few orgasms out, with his mouth.

"Be careful." He helped me out and we turned around to see his mother, Ang, Tech and Maria standing there. Tech was shaking his head but the women gave me a nasty look.

"Bro, you need this." Tech handed him a small bottle of mouthwash. The girls walked me in the bathroom and I cleaned myself up.

"Bitch, did you suck his dick?" Maria asked and handed me a small bottle of mouthwash, too.

"Not yet, but we do kiss after he eats my pussy." They busted out laughing.

"Well take some. I'm sure your husband doesn't want anyone smelling your pussy and I damn sure don't want to." Maria walked out and left me with, Ang and Lizzie.

"Congratulations! I'm happy to have you as a daughter." I thought about Marco's father for a split second. It would've been nice for my kids, to have a grandfather but he messed up. Marco, took his life, the same night he came in the restaurant, starting a bunch of BS. He told me, his father apologized about the shit with Shanta, disrespecting Ang and I, at the hospital and some things from their past. Unfortunately, my husband, was over it and so was I.

"Thank you."

"It's about time, you made it in the family." Ang hugged me.

"I love all of you and thanks for making this day special for me." We all hugged and stepped out. My husband stood there with a grin on his face, waiting for me. I was so in love with him and prayed we lived to be a hundred years old, just to spend more time together.

Marco

"About time you and sis, got married." Tech said and handed me the blunt. After I went in the bathroom to clean myself up, he had me come outside to smoke with him. I knew the ladies would have my wife in there for a long time.

"I know right. Shit, it took us a minute but she's worth it." We stood there finishing the blunt and when we stepped back in, she came out the bathroom, looking as beautiful as ever. I could tell she tried to fix her hair from us, sexing in the carriage. We all lined up outside the ballroom, waiting to be introduced. I could hear the bridesmaids, being called and intertwined her hand in mine.

"I love you Marco."

"I love you too, ma." He lifted my hand and kissed it.

"HERE THEY ARE! MR AND MRS. SANTIAGO." The DJ shouted over the mic. We stepped in and everyone stood, clapping.

"Everyone clear the dance floor, so the new couple, can dance their first song." Rak and I, walked on the floor and the light dimmed, to a purple color.

"Thank you for giving me the perfect wedding."

"It's what you wanted."

"It is but.-" Don't worry about how much it cost. Money will never be an issue. If you or my kids want it, you got it."

"I love you so much, Marco."

"I love you too Rak." I moved her back, turned her around and dipped her.

"I didn't know you knew how to dance like that."

"I don't. The dude off the wedding planner movie did it, so I tried it."

"You know whatttttt?" I shrugged my shoulders and she started laughing.

Once the song went off, I did a dance with my mom and she did one with both, her father and grandfather. Afterwards, the waiters and waitresses started bringing the food out. I glanced around and everyone seemed to be enjoying

311

themselves and I was happy. This is more Rakia's day, than mine and no one was gonna ruin it. Shit, both of our bachelor parties were crashed by haters. The wedding had to go off without any issues.

I had Brielle on my lap, feeding her some mashed potatoes, when Tech, stood up, clinking his glass. The music stopped and everyone stared at him.

"First off, I wanna say Congrats to my brother and his new wife, my sister in law, Rakia." People clapped and you could hear them say, congrats.

"If you knew my brother, you'd know, being married is something he thought only corny people did. His words were always, can't no female ever get me on one knee. Well, I'm here to tell you, he was right. For a long time, I believed he would be lonely forever. That is until Rakia came into his life. Sis, you may not know this but ever since the first day, he saw you at the store, he's been on the hunt for you." I looked at Rak and she covered her mouth.

"No one knew who you were; therefore, he eventually, gave up and said if it's meant to be, it will. Low and behold, you entered the club a year later and he made sure to get your attention. I don't know what you said to him that night, but he said one day you were gonna be his wife and now look. We're sitting here, celebrating the two of you becoming one. Rak, you get the upmost respect from me, for calming him down. And Marco, she is your match bro and there's not a woman out here, I'd rather see you marry and spend the rest of your life with, than her. Congrats bro and I love you." I handed Brielle to a teary eyed Rak and stood up to hug him. He's been by my side through everything and I loved him, like we shared the same parents. Blood couldn't make him anymore, my brother.

"I love you too bro."

"I love you too Tech." Rak hugged him and Brielle reached out for him to take her. She was so damn spoiled by both of us; while lil Tech, was spoiled by my mom, Ang and Rak. After we hugged, Ang stood up and clinked her glass.

"Rakia, I know we had a rocky start as friends and I regret, not taking the time out to get to know you sooner. You by far, are the strongest, caring and most loving woman, I've ever met. You forgave people, who didn't deserve your forgiveness, all because you never wanted to harbor hate and I respect the hell outta you for it." Rak smiled and Ang, looked at me.

"Marco, she was scared to love you and being a man of your stature, she had reason to. However, you were and still are, the light at the end of her tunnel. When you call, or come around, her entire face lights up. She still gets butterflies in her stomach for you. You may get on my nerves, but like my husband said, you two are perfect for one another. I'm glad to call myself, your friend and sister. I wish you all the best." She lifted her glass and so did everyone else. All she had was soda in her cup, like Rak but I guess, a toast is a toast.

Rak, stood up to hug her and so did I. Ang, is right about us getting on each other's nerves but the one thing we had in common, is making sure we loved Rakia. My wife, had a rough life but from here on out, that'll never be an issue.

"Angela Miller, can you come to the dance floor?" The DJ yelled and Tech, handed Brielle back to me. He walked out and told the DJ, to stop the music.

"Baby, what's going on?" I told Rak, to watch. See, Tech rushed to marry Ang, when she came home from school because he thought, she would never come back. He wanted to ask her to renew their vows tomorrow but I told him to do it tonight, in front of everyone. Women loved that shit.

"Tech, what are you doing?" Everyone got quiet. Her parents stood up and lil Tech, ran over to them.

"Ang, you are the woman of my dreams. I love everything about you; even when you're being a spoiled brat. I know we rushed into our first marriage but I wanna do it right, this time." He pulled the box out his pocket. Ang covered her mouth and people started recording.

"You are my forever Ang. Will you marry me again?" He opened the box and it was a huge yellow diamond. He picked it up, at the same place I purchased Rak's. Ang, shook her head yes and he placed it on her finger.

"I'm so happy for them." Rak, kissed my lips.

"Rahmel, is next."

"Oh my God. Really!"

"Yup. Missy's Birthday, is in two weeks. He's having a surprise party and popping the question." She was excited.

"Ma, don't say anything."

"I'm not." She smirked.

"Rak." I gave her a stern look.

"FINE!" She pouted.

"I'll know, if you told ma. It'll show on her face, so keep it a secret."

"I promise."

"You better." We started kissing and someone cleared their throat.

"Can I get a dance with my cousin, or nah?"

"Me or her?" I asked Rahmel being funny.

"I'll take the gorgeous one, for a thousand." Rak, stuck her tongue out and stood. I sat back playing with Brielle and Tech, plopped down next to me. I asked where Ang was, and he pointed to her, talking to Missy and my ghetto ass cousins, showing off her ring.

"Welp! We finally did it. Married men now."

"Yea. It don't seem too different though. I gave her everything already. She just owns me now." We both busted out laughing.

"Marco. Marco." Lil Tech wanted me to pick him up. Brielle pushed him away, though. Tech took my daughter and I picked him up.

"OH MY GOD MARCO!" I heard Rak shout and stood up, quickly. I handed lil Tech, to my mom and went to where she was, crying and hugging some woman. I forgot this lady, was coming. Ang, told me she's the woman, who purchased Rakia's first truck and helped her out, all through high school. They hadn't seen one another since, graduation.

"Marco, this is Ms. Harris. She's my old guidance counselor and.-"

"I know Rak." She shook my hand. I never met her, but anyone who helped my wife, will always be good with me.

"Thank you for coming."

"Thank you for having me." She gave me a hug.

"I'm so happy for you Rakia. You may have heard it already but you deserve happiness."

"Thank you. Let me introduce you to everyone, including my daughter and nephew. I'll be back baby." She pecked my lips and walked off with her. Ang, came and stood next to me.

"What up nigga?" I sucked my teeth.

"Marco, I know we argue a lot, but thank you for being there for Rak. You came in her life and made everything better. The two of you, really are perfect for one another." Tech, came and stood behind her.

"I mean, look at Tech and I. We got married quick and every night, we fuck each other's brains out and.-" I left her standing there.

"WHAT? Marco, don't be like that." I heard her laughing and went to the bathroom. After I finished, I came out the stall and smirked.

"What you doing in here?" I washed my hands and grabbed a paper towel. Since it was a single bathroom, she locked the door and her dress, fell on the floor.

"I'm waiting for my husband, to fuck me in public. Well, not in public, public, but not in private. You think anyone will come in here? Maybe we should.-" I shushed her like always with a kiss and fucked the shit outta my wife, in the bathroom. By the time, we came out, people were starting to leave the reception. I looked at my Rak, after opening the box she handed me.

"You the shit ma." I said, staring at the Rolex watch and airline tickets to China. Call me weird all you want but a nigga wanted to see the Great Wall of China and walk to that mountain, where you can see everything. I had money to do it but never wanted to go alone.

"You like it?" I put the stuff on the table and pulled her in front of me.

"I love it Rak." I lifted her face to look at me.

"Don't ever think, expensive gifts are all I want. Ma, the little things, are just as sentimental." She nodded her head.

"Rak, you have tons of money in your account and I know, you feel like, if you spend it, its like me, buying my own stuff."

"I do."

"Don't think like that. Yes, I gave it to you but others gave it to me."

"What do you mean?"

"In order, for me to be rich, I had to make the money off somebody. Look at it like, you're spending millions of other people's money." She busted out laughing.

"I know, its weird but my money, is your money. Anything you buy, will come from our money. Rak, a man is supposed to provide for his family and I've saved all that money, over the years, for my future wife and kids. I know, everything you do is from your heart and its all that matters, to me."

"How did I get such a good man?"

"Honestly, you're too good for me and I thank God, everyday, you stuck around."

"Marco."

"I'm serious Rak. I thought you'd never speak to me again, after I messed up with that bitch. Thank you for loving me the way you do." I pulled her face to mine and stuck my tongue in her mouth.

"Ok already." I stopped and looked at Ang.

"Tech, lets go so we can fuck all over, like them." I grabbed Rak's hand, our things and walked out the hall. Ang, knew how to make me leave.

"Have fun." My mom yelled, with Brielle in her arms. Rak gave both of them a kiss and, did the same with Ang, Tech and everyone else who came out. I tried to give Brielle back to my mom, and she started having a fit.

"Be good for daddy, Bri." She wasn't tryna hear shit. I opened the door to the limo and we got in.

"That's your fault." She pointed to my screaming daughter, as we pulled off.

"Oh, you don't miss me, when I leave?" She looked at me.

"Every time, baby." She pecked my lips and the two of us, rode to the airport, fondling one another, like most newlyweds. I had my wife by my side, my daughter and a son on the way. My life, couldn't get any better than this.

Epilogue

Two Years Later…

Rakia

"Coming to the stage is a woman, who's not only graduating with every award possible, but also a full-time position at Metal Textiles Corporation, as a Product Development Engineer. I would like to introduce you all to, Mrs. Rakia Santiago." Everyone in the graduation stood and applauded. I walked across the stage, and accepted my degree. It felt like it took me forever to get here, when it didn't. All the hard work, late hours, and taking classes in the summer, paid off. And whether, I needed the money or not, it felt good to start in a position making a lot of it. Ms. Harris, always told me, my mind is what people loved the most about me and she was right.

"Congratulations, Rakia." I shook the hands of all the professors and the Dean, who wrote me a letter of recommendation, for the job. Once they finished their speeches, all of us, tossed our caps in the air. I ran in the back, to grab my things and hurry out to see my family.

"I'm so proud of you ma." Marco handed me a dozen roses. Then placed an erotic and sensual kiss on my lips. Had it not been for Marco Jr. pushing him off me, we'd still be engaged in one. Yes, my son was very protective of me, where Brielle was the same with my husband.

"Daddy, I'm hungry." Brielle was always eating and he gave her, whatever she wanted.

"Ok, lets go eat." See, what I mean. Most likely, he fed them before they got here. You would think my daughter was fat but she was as skinny as could be.

"Congrats, sis." Ang, hugged me and so did Tech.

"Aunty, you did it." Lil Antoine, or as my husband calls him, lil Tech, handed me a small bag. I opened it up and there was a Cartier bracelet in it, that read best friends.

"Ang, you didn't have to."

"It has to match mine." She lifted her arm and showed me the one, I got for her, two weeks ago, at her graduation. I know, people think we stopped going to school, or put it on hold but we didn't. Just because Tina J, didn't mention us going every single day, or how much work we did, doesn't mean, anything. Our men, wouldn't allow us not to finish, even if we wanted to. Hell, it's the reason they chose us, to be their wives.

"Ma, come feed my baby." Marco, took my hand in his and we all walked out.

If you must know, Marco and I, decided to wait on baby number three after my son was born, and now that Marco Junior was turning two shortly, I agreed to our next one. I'm currently pregnant with my second son and Brielle is not happy.

Tech and Ang, are on their fourth kid. He claimed, this one, was an accident but we knew his ass was lying. He wanted a big family, like Marco and wanted to start his sooner, then later. Ang, didn't mind because she said at least, she's still young.

Ang, opened her own boutique and I must say, she's doing very well. People from all over heard about it and if they couldn't get to the store, they ordered online. See, Ang went to NYU for a short time but she never gave up her dream, to make her own clothes. Some are in her boutique and once she sells out, she doesn't make them again. She never wanted too many people rocking the same thing.

Her and Tech, were getting married again, next month. If you're wondering why it took so long, that's easy. Ang, said they were already married and not in a rush. They were one, on paper and he agreed. However, her ass did turn into a Bridezilla and none of us, could wait for it to be over.

Rahmel and Missy, are also on their third child, as well. He popped the question two weeks after my wedding, at her surprise party and of course she said yes. They were married a year later and now he owns, two auto body shops; courtesy of me and my husband. He always wanted his own shop, and since he had my back, growing up, Marco had no problem, opening them up, for him. You should've seen him, when we did a grand opening for the first one. He definitely shed some tears and thanked us, a million times. Everything in there, was top of the line machinery, equipment and anything else he needed to operate, the place. He offered to pay us back, but we wouldn't hear of it. I say we because like my husband said, his money, is my money.

It took me a long time, to spend it but now, I do it with no problem. I still have a separate account my work checks go in, that he knows about. I don't have to touch any of it, but as long as it's there, I feel comfortable. And with this new job, I'll be making even more money. Once I learn more about the business aspect of Engineering, you bet I'm opening my own business. My husband always said, if I want it, I got it and to this day, it's never changed.

I swear, its true when they say, our love is Not Your Ordinary, Hood Kinda Love, because I'm nowhere near hood, yet, my husband is. He has taught me a lot, in these past few years and he'll tell you, the same about me.

Thank you all, for reading our story, falling in love, with our characters, and making us Number #1 on the charts. You are the reason Tina J, continues to write. Look out for the next series, I Just Can't Stop Luvin You. You're guaranteed to fall in love with Cason and Ingrid, too.

THE END

Made in the USA
Monee, IL
18 November 2021

82481307R00184